Three Crowns
and the
Dream Sofa

Three Crowns
and the
Dream Sofa

— LILIANE BROBERG —

Library of Congress Control Number:		2017902233
ISBN:	Hardcover	978-1-5245-9418-3
	Softcover	978-1-5245-9417-6
	eBook	978-1-5245-9416-9

Print information available on the last page.

Rev. date: 02/16/2017

To order additional copies of this book, contact:
Xlibris
800-056-3182
www.Xlibrispublishing.co.uk
Orders@Xlibrispublishing.co.uk
748851

Contents

Chapter 1

The Family

The merry events organised in Viz by the triplet kings made them loved by all. These three brothers were so unalike in appearance, manners, and style of dress that they could be identified with ease wherever they found themselves.

Rather unusually, this day the entire royal family was gathered in one of the gardens for tea. The table was an attractive sight, with food and multicoloured fruits from the rich soil of Viz, and along it resounding chatter could be heard.

"The weather is so stunning I feel like doing nothing today, although I promised the people I would have a city round," exclaimed King Benjamin, often called King II. He had been born half an hour after King Bruno, and work was not his thing. He enjoyed being around people, particularly when he was the centre of attention.

"You're right, the weather is appropriate for relaxing. I'll just chill in the garden after this. How fortunate we are to live in Viz – Land of the Glowing Sun, happy citizens, and no raindrop ever," responded the thoughtful King III. His name was Bernard, and he was born thirty minutes after King Benjamin.

"No one shall go anywhere!" decreed Bruno, who was King I. "We've a meeting just after this. Have you forgotten?" Bruno was the eldest of all the sons and daughters of Queen Ursula Nobel and King Rowel Nobel.

"Oh! A meeting about what?" asked King Benjamin.

"What a question! Does your mind not recall the date on which you were born and that we're organizing a party for that, *monsieur*?" As he responded, King Bruno pointed a finger towards Benjamin, his face red.

"Oh! You mean our birthday?" King Benjamin answered calmly. "You know my help won't make any difference in the preparations. You're very good at juggling several things at a time and taking matters into your own hands. Go ahead and do whatever you wish."

"I'm afraid you won't be going to anywhere," King Bruno answered. "Aren't you ever tired of your city rounds? We've always organised this event together, and we are yet to choose our party theme. So no distractions for now!"

"You can't stop me from doing this," King Benjamin responded, beaming. "I like my city rounds. I love talking to people; this is my reason for being. The joy I get from doing this you can't imagine."

"Yeah, yeah, joy. You simply like being admired during your rounds," sneered King Bruno. "What do you do for these people? Organise Friday pinky parties and fool around with them? I often wonder when you will stop living in your pink cloud."

"Heuuuf! Nonsense," King Benjamin sighed.

"I think we've heard enough. It's all right, Bruno, we'll take part in this meeting," King Bernard answered.

"Holy Saint. No way, I shall not. I have to go to town right away," King Benjamin snapped.

"You won't," King Bruno replied.

"Oh, sure I will. Simply because you're the oldest doesn't mean you can impose your will on me," irritated King Benjamin replied.

"What has birthright got to do with this?" King Bruno retorted. "Now you speak out of context. Anyway, do as you please, and go to your merry-go-round trip, but be informed that I've just rescheduled the meeting for midnight."

"Midnight!" everyone exclaimed.

"Yes, midnight, and this is not questionable. And bring along your birthday speeches, which we shall review," King Bruno said.

"Crazy. You're crazy," replied King Benjamin. "You can't expect us to meet at twelve o'clock at night when we're supposed to be asleep. And besides, it takes so much time and energy to prepare a speech."

"Yeah, for you it takes ages. That is why you should start right now instead of going wandering around town," King Bruno responded.

"Holy Saint, I think you expect and demand too much from yourself and others," said King Benjamin in disgust. "We're not machines that work round the clock, dear brother. Count me out. I won't be there. I'm leaving."

At this, King Bruno stood up and stomped towards the castle, murmuring something like, "My words are indisputable. See you at midnight. *Un point, un trait.*"

"May I be excused as well?" King Bernard asked as he left.

The other table members watched without surprise as the triplet kings departed. Queen Ursula pretended nothing had happened. King Rowel looked worried. Princess Gwendoline pondered on adult behaviour, and Prince Robert Vincent smiled, while Princess Experalda exclaimed in her masculine voice, "Hahahaha! Mum, there go your hilarious sons – the dog, the cat, and the clam. All fools. I informed you that it was a mistake letting these guys be kings, but you never listened. There they are, unable to agree on as simple a thing as organising a birthday party. What more of the affairs of Viz? Hahahaha hahahaha hahahaha!"

As she spoke, the other family members watched Queen Ursula for her reaction, but she was calm as the Pacific Ocean and ignored her daughter's comment.

"Haven't you anything to say?" shouted Princess Experalda. "When will you learn to listen to me?" She kicked Katia, the old cat who stood by her side, as she lifted her imposing, tall, square figure from her seat and stormed off. "I can no longer stand this. Why does she always treat me this way?" Experalda clenched her fists as she murmured and walked towards the castle.

"Mum, wait for me!" cried Princess Gwendoline, running after her.

Three years younger than the triplet kings, Princess Experalda was taller than everyone else in the palace. She wore grey spectacles on her triangular, non-smiling face, and tied her brown hair in a bow that made her look cold and stern. Her dreadful eyes (one was black like that of a snake and the other was yellow-brown like a crocodile's) lit up whenever she was up to something vicious, and then her smile would be twisted. Through it all, she looked beautiful.

In the castle's hallway, Princess Experalda met King Benjamin, who was on his way out. "Experalda," he asked, "may I ask for a favour?"

"What for? I am in no mood for granting one."

"Please, I need your help. You've often done so," he said.

"Go on and be quick," she replied.

"Could you prepare a speech for our birthday party before this night?"

"Oho, I thought you'd decided not to be part of tonight's meeting. Benjamin, learn to keep your word. Why act cowardly? If you say you won't be there, don't be there," Princess Experalda said.

"Don't get me wrong. I said I would not take part in this afternoon's meeting before Bruno rescheduled it to midnight, which still I didn't want. But I changed my mind and want no fuss with Bruno, so my attendance at this midnight meeting will depend on how I feel after my city round. If I don't attend, the least I can do is send my speech for review," King Benjamin responded.

"Well, what do I get in return for helping you?" she asked with a twisted smile.

"What do you want?" King Benjamin asked.

"You know what I want, what I've always desired. Promise me to convince the others, and then will I help you out," Princess Experalda responded.

"Holy Saint, you know it's not easy at all. How can I convince Bruno? I'm sorry, but I can't promise you that," King Benjamin replied.

"Then you won't get any help from me," Princess Experalda said as she climbed the stairs to her quarters. He gaped at her as she went.

She never ceases to surprise me. I cannot deny help to anyone who needs it, particularly if we share the same bloodline. His reflection was interrupted by Princess Gwendoline, who met him in the entrance of the castle. As he came back to himself, he said, "My lovely little princess, how are you today?"

"I'm fine, darling uncle. Are you all right? You seem bothered," Princess Gwendoline said.

"Yes. I was wondering about when to prepare my birthday speech before midnight. Can I ask a favour of you?" King Benjamin inquired.

"Sure," she responded.

"Would you write a speech for me? I know you're a bright little girl."

"Oh yes, yes, Uncle Benjamin! I will. What should I write about?"

"Anything, darling, that has to do with happiness, enjoying life, being good, loving people, etc. etc. Like my speeches during official occasions."

"Okay, I get you."

"You're lovely dear, thank you," he responded.

"Shall I also attend the midnight meeting?" she asked.

"My dear, at that hour, Dreamland angels visit children who are fast asleep and pour upon them a portion of growth so that they can quickly become adults. You wouldn't want to miss that, would you?" King Benjamin replied.

"Yes, I would. Adults have lots of problems that I won't like to partake in. So becoming one ... I'm not so sure of right now. I'd rather be part of your meeting and miss the angels."

"All right, I see. Do you want to know what I'll do for you instead?" King Benjamin asked.

"No, tell me," she responded.

"From now on, you'll be my special guest at my Friday ballroom parties."

"Yippee! Yippee! Yippee! You're the best, Uncle Benjamin. One more thing, though: your ballroom parties are only for grown-ups. I'll have to ask for Mum's permission for that."

"Yes, do so," he responded.

"Will I have to dress in pink like everyone else?" she asked.

"Yes, darling, pink is the dress code," King Benjamin said. "I have to go now, see you later."

"See you, Uncle Benjamin. By the time you are back, your speech will be ready," she responded excitedly. Tenacious like Uncle Bruno when she was at anything, Gwendoline had often desired to be part of her uncles' meetings so as to share with them her brilliant ideas for Viz – but of course, our triplet kings would not grant the wish of this seven-year-old candy eater. Despite this, she still hoped that someday, her plea would be heeded.

In his favourite garden spot under the birch tree, King Bernard lay on the ground mesmerised by the softness of the grass as he intently observed a beetle that leaped from leaf to leaf. A while after came his friend SpyBrow, who he called Spy because he spied and gossiped about everyone in Viz. SpyBrow had a brow on his right eye that was rather unusual.

"Hey there! Is everything okay with you today?" SpyBrow inquired.

"Yes, I'm good," King Bernard replied.

"What were you *thwinking* about?" SpyBrow asked, twisting his thick brow.

"Well, I was thinking about nature, life, and why my toes wiggle," King Bernard replied.

"I *thwink* you should chill a bit. You read too much. How many books did you read today?" SpyBrow inquired.

"Let's see, this morning in the library I read mathematics, philosophy, and a book called *Why Roses Grow*. So in all, three books," he responded.

"Oh la la! My brain would crack if I had to read the way you do daily," SpyBrow said. Changing the subject, he went on, "Those two brothers of yours will never change, I watched the scene this afternoon. They are always disputing on futile matters. Each one feels the need to be right."

"Exactly," King Bernard answered. "Such is life. People have different views and then disagree. So tell me, what is happening in Viz?"

"Nothing special. People are simply excited about the forthcoming birthday celebration," SpyBrow responded.

"Oh, I see, and what do they say?" King Bernard inquired.

"They know it will be grandiose like last year and hope that Queen Ursula will be present this time. They say she's been absent from this event for many years."

"I see. Well, let's hope so," King Bernard responded.

The clock struck midnight and the three kings were all present in their purple meeting boardroom. When King Bruno was about to speak, a knock on the door interrupted him. It was their sister, Princess Experalda.

"To my knowledge, you weren't convened to this meeting," King Bruno said.

"I know that, but I think my presence is needed. Women are well known to be the best organisers, so I'm here to help."

"You're not welcome, madam," proclaimed King Bruno. "Please leave so that we may begin."

"Well, well, well, you'll have to drag me out of here." She made herself comfortable on a seat beside him. "Don't worry, I won't be long. My intention is to get the feel of this uncommon midnight meeting and see how Benjamin copes with his stolen hours of sleep."

King Bruno became impatient and moved towards the door, gesturing his hand towards it. "I repeat, please leave!"

"Gladly, brother. My sleep is too sweet to waste a minute here. See you tomorrow, and hope you guys enjoy your midnight sleep. Oops! Should I say work meeting? Have fun." Her smile was broad as she exited, and King Bernard burst in fits of laughter.

"Let's begin. We've no time to waste," King Bruno said as he quickly took his seat. "May I look at your speeches?"

"Here you are." King Bernard handed his over.

"This is mine." A reluctant and embarrassed King Benjamin handed in his too.

King Bruno quickly read through both speeches and gave his brothers a satisfied look. "I must admit that I'm impressed by your speech, Benjamin. It is brief and straight to the point this time around. Are you getting a hold of it now? With this, you'll spare us the pain of listening to ages of redundant words."

"What do you mean by that?" King Benjamin asked.

"All your official speeches are usually too long, and it'll be good if we don't have to spend hours listening to unnecessary information," King Bruno replied.

"Could I have that speech back? I think I need to read it," King Benjamin said.

"What do you mean you need to read it? You wrote it, didn't you?" King Bruno asked.

"W-e-l-l, never mind, I'll have it as it is," King Benjamin replied.

"Great! If no one has anything else to add, let's move on with the theme for this year. What are your proposals?" King Bruno spoke as he handed the speeches to Earl Wintor, his special advisor.

"'The Kings for the People,'" King Benjamin suggested.

"Okay, it's an idea," King Bruno responded.

"'A New Perspective for Viz,'" King Bernard added in.

"Okay, another option," King Bruno said. "What do you think of 'Long Live the Kings'?" he continued.

"Isn't that a bit clichéd? We need something that motivates the people to believe that we're working for their good," said King Bernard. "'Long Live the Kings' draws all the attention to us instead of the citizens of Viz. It's a bit egocentric."

"That's your opinion, and I think we're already doing them enough good. What more could they ask for? You offer them Saturday Charity Day, during which new clothes are donated to the less fortunate, but the whole town is lined up in front of the castle gates every Saturday morning as though everyone is suddenly become poor. Benjamin organises weekly Friday parties for their entertainment, and I launched Thursday Games Day to make them become skilled hunters. The destitute get fed freely every afternoon in the yellow hall. Moreover, Viz is peaceful, and food grows abundantly even without any hard work from the farmers. We don't ask for taxes as other kingdoms do. I think these people are lazy. And what better future are you talking about? Besides, it's our birthday, so the attention *should* be entirely on us. Benjamin, what do you think of what I just said?" King Bruno asked. "B-e-n-j-a-m-i-n, are you sleeping?"

"E-u-u-h, hmmm, what did you say?" King Benjamin sheepishly asked.

"Monsieur, you've been dozing while we were discussing important matters here," King Bruno pointed out, his reddened cheeks stiffening.

"Sorry, but my brain is completely shut down. What were you saying?" King Benjamin replied.

"I want to know what you think about my theme, as well as the fact that Bernard thinks it's clichéd?"

"*Whatever.* Go on and decide. Ask Earl, isn't he your advisor ..." King Benjamin's voice dragged as he spoke before his face flattened on the table and he dozed even more.

"Pfffff, hopeless," King Bruno sighed.

"Well, it's a good idea to have Earl's opinion, since we're unable to make up our minds," King Bernard pointed out. "One more thing concerning your theme: we'd declared Sunday 'Parish Day,' during which mass attendants thank the Lord for the good deeds of the kings. Isn't that enough praise and recognition? Why want more? Moreover, I still insist on having my theme because I hope

Viz changes for the better through the various endeavours we would have for our citizens so that they can dream again. We've got to keep looking outwards and finding new avenues to accomplish this. Every year since our enthronement, we've done the same thing."

He continued, "You should also know that Viz's citizens are tired of seeing the same three faces during our birthday celebration. They would like to have Queen Ursula in this year's festivity. According to what Spy says, she's been absent from the celebrations for a long time, and her presence will be appreciated by them. Let's do our best to convince her to be part of this."

"Who did you hear this from? Spy?" asked King Bruno with a laugh. "That unknown garden friend of yours? No way. How can I convince her based on an unreliable source of information? You do that yourself. Considering what you said earlier about making the citizens of Viz dream, I don't agree. What do dreams do? They make one lazy. This is a land of hard work. People should learn to work hard, not wait for kings to make them dream. Now let's go on. Earl, what do you think of these three themes?"

"My Lord, for Viz's sake, I think all three recommendations – 'Long Live the Kings,' 'The Kings for the People,' and 'A New Perspective for Viz' – all come down to the same thing," said Earl. "Introducing good change in Viz will not only improve people's lives but will show how engaged you are for their well-being. This will in turn improve the country, because a developed nation is witnessed in the progress of its people. By doing this, you will leave a lasting legacy and be kings who will live forever in the hearts of its people and of future generations. So King Bernard's theme is most appropriate, provided he backs this theme with a solid agenda that will bring about this change, which should be well explained to the subjects during the birthday celebration."

"Okay, tell us, Bernard, what plan do you have for Viz to become better?" King Bruno asked.

"Well, the ideas are still in my mind and are yet to be formulated into a good plan," King Bernard answered.

"Hmm! Okay, let us know once you're through with your plan. That said, the meeting is over. Goodnight," King Bruno concluded. It was past two in the morning.

Chapter 2

Habits Are Difficult to Change

The golden castle of Viz was adorned with diamond roofs, and its gardens emitted nice scents from flowers that made the bees behave gently.

The Rainbow River, endowed with the power to perpetuate life, cut the hilly impressive landscape on the left, and the River of Life on its right flowed with healing virtues. Viz was such a pleasant place to live.

Boredom was non-existent in the palace; it was always bursting with activity. Every morning, each king went about his routine before audience sessions in the afternoons. Three hundred and one members of staff attended the three demanding Kings, each of whom was peculiar in his likes.

The kings met on Monday mornings in their purple boardroom for meetings, which often ended up in quarrels, especially when Princess Experalda took part uninvited. But this first weekday was rather unusual in that all three were gathered in Queen Ursula's and King Rowel's quarters, situated in the eastern side of the castle, far from its chaotic life.

"Please go on, Bernard," said Queen Ursula.

"The citizens of Viz would appreciate your presence during the birthday celebrations," King Bernard explained. "It's been a long time since they saw you."

"You know," she told her son, "I am no longer on duty as queen, and I strive to stay away from the affairs of Viz. This brain of mine has gone through so much hassle over the years that it needs to relax now. Rather, tell me about how you are doing. I am more interested in your well-being. Bruno informed me of an unknown friend of yours who provides you with doubtful news about Viz. Who is that?" Queen Ursula inquired, her sharp eyes twinkling with wisdom.

"Doubtful, not at all. It's my friend Spy, and ..." King Bernard began.

"Hahahahaha! His friend Spy. Hahahahaha, Spy, the imaginary bird. Hahahahaha, he now has bird friends. *Mon Dieu* ... Hahahahaha," King Bruno burst in.

"Hahahahaha!" King Benjamin joined in the laughter. "That garden is doing you no good, Bernard. I'm beyond words. You guys say I live in a pink world, but I would rather remain in it than hear words from an imaginary thing. With all reason, this is not a suitable way to collect information, especially when it concerns this kingdom. You know that all t-o-o w-e-l-l, Bernard. Fetching information from a bird! This can't compare to the news I get while on city rounds, which is more authentic because people keep me abreast of all the happenings in Viz. Hahahahaha, you become so ridiculous when you come up with this bird stuff. Spend less time in the library, too, because reading makes you crazy." King Benjamin almost choked with laughter as he wiped a tear from his eye with his pink handkerchief.

"You brag too much, *monsieur*," said King Bruno. "The gossip you get from town is as worthless as the information from Bernard's imaginary bird. When your town trips cease being for ego purpose, then shall we obtain concrete information from you. I must admit that it's hilarious living with you both. Bird and people fanatics. Hahahahaha," King Bruno laughed loudly.

"Now you're not being fair," King Benjamin retorted.

"Quiet, both of you! Bernard was still talking, and was interrupted with your usual show. What have you done to help him out of this situation? Have you shown empathy?Mockery of someone does not make you better. And this displays your stupidity, because you judge based on your ignorance of the bigger picture. Two crucial words for you two: ' Always listen.' So now, allow him to express himself." At Queen Ursula's direction, the laughter stopped.

After they had conversed with their mother for hours, the sons left her quarters with good news: She would partake in the celebration.

Daily, people sought for counsel from the kings for personal, family, or financial matters. Most audience sessions were chaotic, because the triplet kings disagreed on solutions to issues. Subjects with problems were amazed at this and returned home saddened by the fact that their problems remained unsolved. Year in and year out, the situation worsened. As people realized they would receive no help from the kings, fewer even requested an audience.

One Wednesday afternoon in April, a small audience sat in wait for the kings who would judge the day's case. As the triplet kings entered the throne room, the noisy crowd of supporters stopped arguing. The kings sat on their seats and gently clapped their hands to direct Earl to read the day's case.

"Mr Ullord Brimgard, a farmer residing in Viz, complains this day about Mr Ringman Orwell, resident shepherd of Viz. Mr Ullord desires a compensation for his crops, damaged last Saturday in his farm by ..." Earl's reading was interrupted by the sound of an opening door. It was Princess Experalda, who walked into the room accompanied by two servants and ushered them to place her throne besides King Bernard's.

"What do you think you're doing?" asked King Bruno as his face reddened.

She ignored his question and simply sat on her throne, stared at him with her glasses placed on her nose tip, and said, "Your face looks like an apple. Earl, you can proceed with the day's matter." She continued as though no question had been asked.

Confused, Earl glanced at King Bruno for instruction and was gestured by him to go on.

"The day's case is about Mr Ullord Brimgard, who desires to be compensated for his crops that were damaged by Mr Ringman's sheep that ventured into his farm last Saturday. Mr Ringman refuses to compensate him and says Mr Ullord has no evidence that his sheep ate his crops. Mr Ullord confirms that he witnessed Mr Ringman's flock leave their barn for his farm. End," Earl concluded.

"Come forward, Mr Ullord and Mr Ringman. Do you have witnesses to ascertain both of your claims on what happened?" King Bernard asked.

"No, my Lord!" Mr Ullord and Mr Ringman responded at the same moment.

"My Lords, if I may speak, this is just a framed-up story. Mr Ullord is envious of my doing so well with the sheep-rearing. Meanwhile, his farming produce is not as good," said Mr Ringman.

"You old liar, I'm not jealous of your success," said Mr Ullord.

"Yes you are," responded Mr Ringman

"No I'm not," answered Mr Ullord.

"Please stop this comedy. We'll pay for your lost crops. How much do you evaluate your loss at?" inquired King Benjamin.

"*Mon Dieu*. What a bad way to solve this matter," interrupted King Bruno.

"Why is it not a good way? Neither of them has a witness to confirm who did what. So now to end this quarrel, we pay for Mr Ullord's lost crop," King Benjamin argued.

"Does this method really solve the problem? I don't think so," King Bruno replied.

"Do you've a better idea?" King Benjamin asked.

"Solving this matter as such will be costly for us, and later on, more people will frame up similar stories and expect us to compensate them – which is not good," King Bruno said.

"Then tell us how to solve this. You seem to know better than anyone. All I know is that so far, my solution is best," King Benjamin spoke sarcastically.

"No it isn't," King Bruno argued back, and then an argument started between the two kings while the crowd watched in amazement. At this scene, Princess Experalda laughed so loudly that her voice echoed all over the palace. King Bernard observed in silence.

"This is the easiest solution to end this quarrel," said Princess Experalda sharply. "All of Mr Ringman's sheep should be slaughtered, and then they both will be equal in their loss. No one will be jealous of the other, and this shall not be costly for us."

"No, please, don't do that, my lady. I'll compensate Mr Ullord for his lost crops," Mr Ringman begged.

"Problem solved! It shall be as you've spoken, and if we still hear about this dispute, you know what awaits your flock. The audience is now over. You may leave. Tomorrow is another day," concluded Princess Experalda.

She stood up with a triumphant look on her face, elated at how swiftly she had settled the matter. The whole room stood as well, and the audience left.

As she beamed with joy from ear to ear, her brothers simply stared at her in displeasure. So did Earl, who hated what he'd just seen and resolved to himself to put an end to this behaviour. *In honour of my oath to serve Queen Ursula, King Bruno, and Viz, I'll not* let these boys perish from their ignorance. Queen Ursula must intervene! he thought.

Earl was a retired servant of Queen Ursula's time, and King Bruno had engaged him as his counsellor for official matters, which displeased the other two kings. They thought it was an unequal share of staff members, since each king had been assigned one hundred servants and now Bruno had one extra. They had made their displeasure known and advised him to retire Earl, since he almost never used the man's service.

Stubborn and opinionated as always, King Bruno usually argued that Earl was useful for his rule. Whenever he defended himself this way, the two others laughed their lungs out, because Bruno was an autocratic ruler.

Some time after, Earl went into his office, for he needed to reflect on what had just happened. No sooner did he sit than he became lost in thought. *This is becoming unbearable, what should I do to end this conflict among the little boys?* This is how he called them whenever he was angered by their behaviour. *And this Princess Experalda who keeps playing her brothers to fight each other – how can I stop this?*

Earl grew weary as he brooded on these issues and recalled how once Viz was a haven of diplomatic affairs. During that time, Tuesdays were his glorious days, because he fully assumed his diplomatic role as important guests visited Viz for deals of all sorts. Unfortunately, the erratic behaviour of the triplet kings had ended most noble relations, leaving Viz with few allies due to various diplomatic scandals.

He recalled how once King Benjamin had been assigned a negotiation deal with the hard-to-please King Mathew of Vasso. Unprepared for this meeting because he had feasted an entire week, Benjamin mistook the man for King Keneth of Riz, and also confused the purpose of their negotiation. Aggravated by this, King Mathew of Vasso thereafter disconnected from all friendly ties with Viz.

On another occasion, King Bruno chased King Henry XIV with his entourage from Viz because he had disrespected Bruno's authority. No one really knew what happened except Earl, who had pleaded with him to remain serene during their hard exchange. Since King Bruno could not reckon with composure, Earl's plea was not heeded.

Apart from his garden and books, King Bernard had abstained from all royal engagements.

Brooding on the way the boys ruled always gave Earl a headache. He was afraid for Viz because in his opinion, its resources were being wasted and crucial matters remained unattended.

Unfortunately, Queen Ursula remained undisturbed whenever he informed her of her sons' behaviour. In her opinion, she had done her time, and it was now the boys' era.

"There is surely a way out, surely there is," he murmured to himself.

Wonder if my birthday will one day be an official feast? Why do my brothers always have the best meat and I barely have the remains? It shouldn't be this way. I'll someday have my way, Princess Experalda thought as she observed how King Bruno ordered staff around in preparation for the birthday party.

Bruno was obsessed with making this event more grandiose than the year before, especially with Queen Ursula's participation. News of her attendance had reached all the corners of Viz.

He was so engaged that his brothers had very little to say in the organization, and often his busy nature was likened to his big hands and feet, which needed to be all over the place. Others joked that he rose up first in the morning and went last to bed – after midnight when everyone was fast asleep, even palace staff members – because of this busy nature. Some said it was because he was born at the exact time the sun rose, so he rose with it.

"You're doing a great job here," King Benjamin told King Bruno as servants ran about in obedience to his orders. Plants were trimmed, and corners were polished and decorated. Earl was in charge of invitations, and Maria was involved with the menu planning.

"I've a suggestion: Could you add more flowers at the entrance where we'd welcome royal guests? They should be pink to make it more beautiful," King Benjamin proposed.

"This is not a pink birthday party," King Bruno responded.

"It's our birthday, and I've a say in this matter too," King Benjamin pointed out.

"Wait for your Friday parties, and you can decorate it as you like," King Bruno replied.

"This is becoming too mu—" King Benjamin did not finish as King Bernard chimed in.

"Please calm down. This is a happy event, so no fights. Benjamin, allow Bruno to continue with the preparations. He has always done this."

"No, I want to be involved as well. Mum should know that I too took part in the preparations. I would like to—" King Benjamin insisted. King Bernard left the scene for his favourite garden spot, as he sensed a dispute about to start between his brothers.

In the garden, SpyBrow was happy to see him and zealous to inform him of the latest news.

"Princess Experalda is up to something suspicious. A disguised person left her apartments some time ago," the bird tweeted.

"Don't mind Experalda. She is bored and always up to something," King Bernard responded.

"And don't you care? You should inform your brothers."

"You know I've reported to them on several occasions every crucial matter you kept me aware of. Unfortunately, I've been naive to think they would believe in your existence. I've had my share of mockery, so from now henceforth, no more information-sharing with them. Concerning Experalda, let her do what she pleases. It's never grave, and you can't stop people from being who they are and doing what they want."

"You're hopeless in your reasoning. Does anything ever bother you?" SpyBrow asked.

"Yes, things do, but not this kind," King Bernard responded.

Queen Ursula was much acclaimed by the crowd of Viz who feasted in the garden as she waved and walked past them on the red carpet that led into the castle.

She had forgotten how good it felt to be showered with praise, and her face glowed with delight. Never an emotional person, she felt tears of joy gush down from her eyes as she recalled the day she had ceded her throne to her triplet sons on her sixtieth birthday. She had wanted it to be memorable, since on that same day, they had turned twenty-seven. Thereafter, in honour of that unforgettable event, her sons had ordained their birthday and hers an official feast day.

Now retired senior citizens, the former queen and her husband spent their days on travels round the world. Apart from several visits paid to relatives and friends living in other kingdoms, including her younger sister Queen Malgory, who was married to the King of Gothen, they had seen almost all the countries in the five continents.

It was three o'clock in the afternoon, and in no time, the palace had become like a bee's nest as the guests arrived one by one. Viz's royalty welcomed them at the entrance of the castle. Though some of these invitees had been to Viz's palace on several occasions, they never ceased to marvel at its immensity, with more than fifty floors filled with four hundred bedrooms (rumour had it there were one thousand). Once in, people got lost in countless rooms, which they tried to label as they took the tour: the Russian Roulette room (where secret discussions were held); the knights' hall that held gigantic receptions; the red dining room; the pink ballroom that received subjects during Friday parties; three big kitchens in which meals were prepared for the royal family, festivities, and the poor; and so many, many more.

As was customary during feasts, people marvelled at anything, whether it was impressive or not. So did they for the birthday theme, which was spelled out on banners: "Long Live the Kings."

With an unfailing composed demeanour and a twisted smile (which caught King Bernard's attention, since she was not a smiley person), Princess Experalda greeted invitees. Her brother wondered what she was up to this time and attentively observed how she imposed herself as though one of a ruling foursome. As she stood in the fifth position at the entrance of the hall, she took advantage of her height as guests showed up from a distance and called after them from where she stood as they waited in line to greet King Bruno, who was lined up first in the welcoming committee. This created a confusing scene, since some invitees did not know who to pay their attention to, as King Bruno struggled to have her quieted while he greeted them.

So it was with Princess Experalda, who always tried to have her way. Rumour had it she cared for no one but herself.

Experalda's daughter, Princess Gwendoline, was not named after her father, Prince Robert Vincent, since he was not of royal descent. Experalda had desired instead the royal name Noble. Queen Ursula objected, but still Experalda named the girl Noble, which worried the least Prince Robert Vincent, a gentleman and a great academic. Princess Experalda hoped his wit would serve her purpose someday as she aspired to a brighter future.

A few hours later, all entertained guests were deep in conversation as a velvet dressed servant announced that speeches would be made by the kings. At this, everyone gathered by the podium mounted for that purpose. Immediately, as King Bruno stood up to speak, a royal presence with his noble delegation of ten people was heard making a scene in the hallway.

"Is there no one in Viz polite enough to receive me and my entourage? Why was I invited in the first place? This is so rude. I demand an immediate apology," shouted King Mathew of Vasso. Confused, King Bruno looked towards Earl, who was even more confused as he searched for an explanation.

"No one has invited you, intruder," King Bruno responded as he swiftly recollected himself.

"Deplorable you, I hold my invitation here at hand which reads:

King Bruno, King Benjamin, and King Bernard
Along with former Queen Ursula
Request the pleasure of your company at the castle of Viz
to celebrate
Their thirty-seventh and seventieth birthday
A Royal Feast to be held
On the 19th day of April, at 3:00 p.m.

As he finished reading, he handed the invitation to Earl, who suddenly realized who might have done this. King Bernard, in shock, turned towards Princess Experalda, whose twisted smile had grown broader.

Immediately, like bushfire, those present whispered in each other's ears. To avoid a greater scene, Queen Ursula approached

King Mathew, calmed him down, and offered him her seat. She instructed Earl to ensure that his noble company were well seated too. As though nothing had occurred, she gestured to King Bruno to go on with his speech, which he did with a blushing face. His speech was shorter than planned, and King Bernard's also. But faithful to himself, King Benjamin took his time as he read his with excitement.

"People of Viz," he began, "life is enjoyable, we all know that. I am so happy to share with you this joyful event which marks that beautiful spring day when I was born. So, rejoice with us," King Benjamin read and winked at Princess Gwendoline, who nudged her mum's leg as she felt proud while he read.

Then he went off script, "May I add these few words, my lovable guests?" King Benjamin spoke on completely unshaken by King Bruno's frown and the amused look on the face of King Bernard, who was thinking, *Benjamin is now in his pink cloud. He just says the same thing all over.*

Oblivious of time, Benjamin kept on talking, almost going to an hour. Finally he said, "On an ending note, life is roses, and no thorn should make the roses less lovely. Happy birthday to us and you, we Kings for the People." King Benjamin finished and the crowd applauded, happy that finally they would go on with the feast. During official events, while he gave his speeches, no one dared to interrupt for fear of having these last longer.

The rest of the evening went on as planned. People enjoyed the food, drinks, and musical entertainment. Even King Mathew of Vasso seemed appeased.

When most guests had left at the end of the ceremony, Earl handed out a letter to each of the triplet kings. They read it in their beds that night:

> My Dear Lords,
>
> With all due respect, I hope that these few words find a place in your hearts.
>
> A long time ago, I swore to serve Viz honourably, and in all sincerity, I had hoped that once enthroned, your rule would be more glorious than the preceding one. Unfortunately, my expectations failed me.

I fear for Viz, for it might become vulnerable to lurking enemies with regards to the numerous scandals we have had, the way resources are dilapidated on exuberant events, the incessant quarrels during audiences despite my unheeded advice for each king to take turns in solving people's issues, and the neglected pending affairs of Viz.

It is my fervent prayer that we never become entangled in the dangerous traps that lie ahead of us due to ignorance, unpreparedness, and disorientated ruling, for our enemies grow stronger by the day.

With all due respect, all I demand is understanding and unity among you brothers, so that we can work together towards a stronger Viz.

Your fervent servant,
Earl Wintor

The next morning during a debriefing about the feast, the kings expressed their appreciation for Earl's good advice, but he was soon disappointed as he struggled to bring their attention to a pending issue about a court case. They were interested only in discussing the best dressed guest at the party. It was not long before the meeting ended on their discord about this subject. Earl was so downcast such that he contemplated submitting his resignation.

In the afternoon, Earl met Princess Experalda in the Russian Roulette room for a short meeting.

"I know what you did last night," Earl said.

"Yes, and it's just a warning to all of you who underestimate me," she responded.

"Viz is like an egg about to crack and needs no feud but everyone's support to make it stand strong," Earl said.

"Let it crack then, and I can promise that it will fall apart if I don't obtain what I want. Mum should have ordained me king the day she enthroned those three fools."

"You were twenty-four then, and the law forbids anyone below twenty-five from being considered for ruling," Earl replied.

"Then why was Mum enthroned at the age of eighteen? Why was it different for her?"

"The constitution was different during your Mum's time, and some years after. Just before she had kids, it was changed."

"I am over twenty-five now, and I can rule," snapped Experalda. "What I've learned in life is that when rulers want stuff done in their interest, they change things. This can be done for me as well if they really want it. Nevertheless, I won't waste my time being deterred from my path by you. Remind my mum and my absent-minded brothers of my intention to rule with them. Since no one listens to me, tell them that at all costs, I *will* get to the throne of Viz someday."

At this, she left the room, banging the door on her way out. But her steps were slowed as she met Princess Gwendoline, who had been standing by the door caressing Katia the cat in wait of her. Katia purred, leaped from Princess Gwendoline's hands, and ran for her life.

"Mum, you don't have to be mean to get what you want. Especially when you deal with family," Princess Gwendoline said, for she had overhead the conversation.

"My family is you and your dad. The rest are relatives. You're too young to understand the intricacies of power. Let's go," Princess Experalda said as they mounted the stairs that led to their luxurious living quarters. In their entrance hall were portraits drawn by Princess Gwendoline of parents, grandparents, and relatives which Princess Experalda prided herself in.

Seven-year-old Princess Gwendoline was unlike her mum. Kind-hearted and too talkative, she reasoned like adults and gave lessons to her friends who misbehaved. This brown-haired, chubby, pink-cheeked girl always finished her plate of food; spoke English, French, Bantu, and Japanese; and played the piano like Mozart. Mathematics was her favourite subject at school, and she wore pink at home every time she had these lessons.

Chapter 3

The Dispute

A season had gone by, and summer approached. Life in the castle went on as usual. Nothing had changed.

It was a Monday morning just like every other hot day, beautified by the immaculate blue sky filled with dotted clouds. The triplet kings debated in their purple room on current affairs.

Suddenly, King Benjamin burst out in anger. "I don't think you're right, Bruno, always overpowering. I don't like that."

"Oh yeah, think you should have it, Mr Pinky?" King Bruno replied.

"You sit around giving orders boisterously, which doesn't make you right," King Benjamin shouted back.

Dismayed, King Bernard stared at these fellows and left for some quiet time in his favourite garden spot, for he could not handle it any longer.

Why do my brothers always disagree? Arguing over a coat as if it were crucial for organizing the Royal Midsummer Festival. Hmm, humans will never cease to intrigue me, he thought. He got lost in his thoughts until SpyBrow interrupted him some moments later.

"Hey there, what're you *thwinking* about?" SpyBrow asked. His blue colour glowed as he perched on a birch branch. "I was loitering round the corner when I saw you sitting by the tree," he continued.

"Hey, Spy, how are you? Nothing special on my mind, just my brothers with their usual scenes. Tell me, what have you been up to lately, or what is happening in town?" King Bernard inquired.

"Everyone is excited about the upcoming Royal Midsummer Festival organized by the kings. It's the talk of the town. Many think the weather will be warm, while others think it shall be cold," SpyBrow spoke excitedly.

"Oho, this reminds me to consult the weatherman," King Bernard exclaimed.

"You mean that multicoloured-dressed guy, Elix Newman, who confuses red for orange?" SpyBrow whistled. Just then a bell rang – it was lunchtime.

"Sorry to end our conversation here. I feel hungry now. Talk to you some other time," concluded King Bernard.

"Hmm, mmm, mmm! This is very delicious, Maria," praised King Bernard.

Maria was the chief cook of the palace. In her mid-fifties, she had shiny grey hair that brightened her face. Her lips were slightly deformed to the right due to her constant smile. She wore a light-blue apron embroidered with golden threads.

Nothing ever bothered Maria, not even the miserable months she had spent when the kings complained about her food. That year, she cooked badly due to a severe hand injury which had her mix all the ingredients in her soup without measure. Fortunately, the kings called for Dr Wellington (the best osteopath), who prescribed some medication that took the pain away. Before then, in her attempts to get well, she drank water from the River of Life, which did not help because she did not believe in it enough for it to heal her.

She smiled as she served the apple pie. Despite her delicious fish soup that both kings Bruno and Benjamin enjoyed, neither of them said a word and they simply stared at each other in anger, which worsened the unusual silence in the red dining room. From all indications, they were still mad at each other following the morning's quarrel.

To cheer this cold atmosphere, King Bernard said, "I spoke with Spy today, and he said the whole city is excited about the upcoming Royal Midsummer Festival we shall be organizing." His words had no effect. Whenever he mentioned SpyBrow in any conversation, his brothers always teased him in amusement, but this time around, it was not the case. *This is serious*, King Bernard thought.

"I heard there was a quarrel this morning over a useless item. Is that true?" inquired Princess Experalda as she looked in the kings' direction. No one said a word, and so she kept on talking. "What was it all about?" Still, nobody responded.

Princess Gwendoline, who was back from school for her lunch break, looked up in bewilderment from her plate of mashed potatoes.

"It's all right if you don't feel like talking about it," said Princess Experalda, "but remember this: the strongest one will win this cause. Only fools lose. Hope you remember that, hahahahaha! You guys look so hilarious." Princess Experalda smiled, conscious of what she was doing.

At her words, King Bernard felt a tensed atmosphere as his brothers exchanged dark looks.

"No, Mum, I think you're wrong," Princess Gwendoline broke in. "The wisest person always wins. Not necessarily the strongest. Letting go doesn't make one a fool but rather the wise one, because it shows an understanding of ill human behaviour. I don't care about the reason for Uncle Bruno and Uncle Benjamin's quarrel, but I think they should both let go of their hurt and pride and reconcile instead. Oh! now I should hurry back to school. Don't want to be late for my geography class." And with that, Princess Gwendoline scurried out of the room.

Chapter 4

A Welcome Visit

As the days went by before the festival, Kings Bruno and Benjamin avoided each other like a dog and cat. They took opposite directions when they came each other's way. The situation grew worse, despite King Bernard's efforts to reconcile them. Needless to say, Earl's plea for peace was in vain.

News had gone out that the kings were at war and the festival was to be cancelled. This caused people to request more audiences just to verify that the rumours were true, and the kings were not in the mood to listen to people's issues.

The feud among the two brothers continued and spoiled the peaceful atmosphere that had reigned in the castle. It was so bad that King Bruno spent his days in his study, avoiding King Benjamin, who spent his time sleeping instead of chatting as he usually did. He was not used to such strife.

With the ongoing feud, there was every indication that the Royal Midsummer Festival would not be held in Viz as was the custom. It was an event which always drew several royal invitees and crowds from Viz and neighbouring kingdoms, and the three kings always planned it.

As he relaxed in his bath, King Bernard stared at the ceiling, wondering how he could solve this feud between his estranged brothers and was also burdened by the fact that the festival was approaching and so little had been done in preparation. Fortunately, Earl had taken charge of running the castle, since King Bruno was so disinterested.

Just as King Bernard was about to get out of his bath, an idea popped out. "Now I know what to do!" he whispered under his breath as he quickly scrubbed himself with a loofah. "Bohr, could I have my towel please?"

Bohr, the master in charge of baths, ushered in a bath attendant, who brought along an organic lime green towel and handed it to King Bernard. Afterwards, King Bernard dressed up and later secretly discussed his plan with Earl and Princess Gwendoline.

A few days later, Queen Malgory arrived at Viz before teatime. While her luggage was taken upstairs to one of the royal guest rooms, she said "Good heavens! I feel so dirty after this long journey and would like to freshen up before going down for tea. Would Bohr assign some lady attendants to prepare a sweet bath for me? I want it filled with honey, milk, and these aromatic oils from Egypt, which fortunately I didn't forget this time as I had done during my previous visit. Good heavens! How unclean I felt then, despite the fact that I took five baths daily. I'm nothing without my sweet aromas."

Queen Malgory had always received invitations from the triplet kings to the Royal Midsummer Festival, though this time around she had noticed only King Bernard's signature was on hers. She found this strange. Her husband, the king of Gothen, could not make it due to his busy schedule with the affairs of his kingdom.

Her invitation had been accompanied by an urgent note from King Bernard requesting her presence. She could not say no, since she loved spending time with her beloved ones. Queen Malgory was ten years younger than her sister Queen Ursula. Some attributed her ageless, acclaimed beauty to genetics, while others said it was due to her strict beauty regimen of essential oils.

She had a long straight nose, fluffy brown hair that touched her back, and marine blue eyes that charmed anyone who looked at them.

When she was a young lady, before she got married, kings and princes of different kingdoms desired her for a bride, but her father, King Benedict Pontus, was very selective regarding who merited her for wife. He thus organized unending contest challenges for her would-be husband. King Winberg, then prince of Gothen, had proved himself valuable.

Just before tea, Princess Gwendoline tapped on King Benjamin's door, just as King Bernard had instructed her.

"Who is it?" a feeble voice answered from the room.

"It's me, Gwendoline, uncle."

"Oh! Sweetie, what can I do for you?" inquired King Benjamin.

"We're organizing the Friday ball today. Could you come down to see the decorations?"

"Hmm, what day is it? OMG! It's not even Friday. Why do you organize it now, and by the way, who is *we*?" King Benjamin inquired.

"*We* is Mum and I," Princess Gwendoline responded.

"Oh no, not your mum. Wait for me, let me see this," King Benjamin exclaimed.

King Benjamin was a lover of parties, and this pink dancing day had been his idea. Needless to say, Princess Gwendoline usually insisted on being invited (following their letter deal with Benjamin), the reason being that pink was her best colour, and since Fridays were pinky, she had to be a guest. This thrilled her favourite uncle, who then had her as a special invitee. Princess Experalda, on the other hand, was quite displeased. She rather preferred her daughter to concentrate on her homework, but she failed at this on Fridays.

Meanwhile, at another door, there was another knock.

King Bruno growled from his study, "Who dares to disturb me at this hour of the day?"

"It's simply me – Bernard. May I request a minute of your time, please?"

"Enter, the door is open."

"I will be brief: Aunt Malgory is here," King Bernard said as he entered the room.

"Aunt Malgory is here? For what reason? Is she all right?" King Bruno inquired in surprise.

"I don't know," King Bernard replied. "She asked for you and is waiting in the Russian Roulette room."

"Okay, I'll be there in a minute. Wait for me, I'm coming down with you," King Bruno exclaimed. He quickly made himself presentable, and off they went.

As they arrived downstairs, King Bruno frowned as he saw King Benjamin, who was chatting with Queen Malgory. But with his aunt there he could not go on his way, so he sat down next to her. As King Bruno settled into an armchair, he overheard King Benjamin joking about how Princess Gwendoline had tricked him into coming downstairs. King Bruno then understood that King Bernard had done the same for him. He stared at his brother warningly, and King Bernard, knowing what this look was, simply smiled.

They all loved Aunt Malgory, for she was always jovial and kept everyone in a good mood. While having tea, they chatted for hours, and as nature did its thing, King Bruno and King Benjamin started speaking to each other as though there had never been any strife.

This was so pleasing to King Bernard, who rejoiced at the fact that his plan had worked out as expected. He knew that Queen Malgory's visit would bring a happy end to this feud.

Their aunt remained unaware of the feud between her two nephews.

"Aunt Malgory," said King Bernard, "your presence makes us happy, and I'm glad you quickly came as soon as I asked for you. The reason I'd wanted you earlier, before the festival, is because these two nephews of yours have been in a fight for almost two months."

"Good heavens! Why? Don't make me age before my time. Buns and Beans, what has been the issue with you guys? Can't you live in peace for one second?"

"Your Buns and Beans have had a fight over who was to wear the coat during the Royal Midsummer Festival, and not any kind of coat – the one which Ingrid found last year in an abandoned room," King Bernard explained.

"Do you mean the lost but found Multicoloured Coat?" she inquired.

"Hahahaha! Yes," King Bernard answered.

"What? Hahahahaha hahahahaha hahahahaha! Cute little boys. Aren't you aware that it can't fit either of you? Buns would tear it to pieces, and Beans would swim in it. Hahahahaha hahahahaha hahahahaha!" Queen Malgory laughed heartily.

Finally Queen Malgory wiped her teary eyes with a handkerchief and said, "Now let's be serious. The Multicoloured Coat of golden embroideries dates thousands of generations back, and it had been entrusted by my great-grandfather, King Edward I Pontus, to the care of King Edward II Pontus, my grandfather. Both had ruled with admirable wisdom, and people said this was partly due to their possession of this coat. It was believed that the Multicoloured Coat could empower anyone who wore or owned it, and this made everyone covet it. A myth exists that only the chosen one believed to be the Bearer can have it on, and no one until that date will if this is true," Queen Malgory said.

King Bernard, exhilarated by the revelation about the coat, began to question its disappearance and sudden reappearance. He thought it was weird that during the previous years, Ingrid had not

38

discovered it during her cleaning inspections. *Did someone hide it there?* he wondered. She had claimed that it had been found in one of the chambers of the ancestral treasure room. His brains now worked.

As he went to bed that night, he was elated because his brothers had reconciled – and equally happy for what he had learned about the Multicoloured Coat. This was an answer to the many questions he had asked his mother and Ingrid about why the coat could not be given to a charitable cause. His mother, Queen Ursula, whom he always sensed carried some secrets, simply told him off and advised him to concentrate on becoming a better leader. He had wondered how on earth her response was related to his queries about the Multicoloured Coat.

Before going to bed that evening, the family enjoyed a serene dinner as kings Bruno and Benjamin promised to respect one another. Queen Malgory's presence had a great effect on everyone, even on Princess Experalda, who behaved well that night.

News went out that day that the kings had reconciled.

Chapter 5

The Royal Midsummer Festival

T he Royal Midsummer Festival was an event that kept the kingdom of Viz active. On its eve, parents with their kids decorated the midsummer pole in the afternoons while bonfires were lit in the evenings. Girls kept under their pillows seven flowers harvested from the fields and dreamt of their would-be husbands.

Everyone was excited about the festival. Even neighbouring kingdoms took part in this event. As was the custom in Viz, the festivities were flamboyant.

On midsummer day, Gwendoline woke up very early, worried about the fact that she had no orange hat to match the orange dress she would wear for the event.

During breakfast in the red dining room, she recounted her misery about the hat, while her mother said, "Gwendy, finish up your tea, your maths tutor will be here in thirty minutes."

"Oh no, not today. It's midsummer. Shouldn't I enjoy like everyone else?"

"Yes, you will, only after completion of your assignments," Princess Experalda said.

"Oh! This is so unfair. I want to take it easy today," Princess Gwendoline exclaimed in dismay.

"Assignments are engines that make your brains work, and the more your practice, the better you'll become in class," Princess Experalda responded.

"I'm already the best pupil in class," Princess Gwendoline said.

"Don't argue, little girl. No assignments, no Midsummer Festival for you," Princess Experalda said in a threatening voice.

At her mother's words, Princess Gwendoline said nothing more and sulked silently.

"Oh la la la la la la! Experalda, you're hopeless. Allow our darling princess to enjoy the midsummer," King Benjamin said in defence of his favourite niece. "She works so hard at school. Shouldn't you be happy for that? I never did as well as her in school and spent time daydreaming during lessons and usually scored zero in maths and other subjects, but here I am today, most-liked king of Viz, Oh, *que la vie est belle.*"

"Yeah, and what a king you are!" Princess Experalda mocked.

"Oho, hahahahaha, good heavens! *Ma cherie*, don't be sarcastic to your brother," Queen Malgory said. "Little darling, don't worry. I think I've an orange hat in one of my boxes. I'll give it to you," she continued as she sipped hot coffee.

"Thank you, Grand-Aunt Malgory!" Gwendoline cheered.

"Why couldn't you get a hat before?" King Bernard inquired.

"The hat weaver had run short of raw materials," Princess Gwendoline answered.

"Shouldn't ladies have flower crowns instead of hats during midsummer?" King Bernard questioned.

"Yes, but I'd rather have an orange hat with orange flowers round it. I don't like the crown of thorns. They hurt my scalp. I'm starting a new style," Princess Gwendoline responded.

"But why orange and not pink or red or blue?" King Bernard went on.

"Orange makes me happy," Princess Gwendoline answered.

"But you like pink, don't you? Why not pink then?" King Bernard continued.

"Yes I do, but orange is a warm, sunny colour, which I think goes well with midsummer," Princess Gwendoline replied.

"Hahahaha! Then you should have yellow instead of orange. Yellow looks more like the sun," King Bernard said.

"Yes, yellow looks more like the sun, but orange is merrier, and midsummer is a merry event, so I wear orange!" Princess Gwendoline said.

"Hahahaha! OK, you win, Gwendy. I like challenging your intellect," King Bernard said.

They both laughed as King Bruno watched silently, not interested at all in this conversation. He had more important concerns at hand than talk about orange hats.

After breakfast, Princess Gwendoline collected her assignments from her tutor but did not work on them. She instead adorned the orange hat given to her by Queen Malgory with orange flowers, with the help of her nanny, Magarette.

Several guests arrived in the afternoon for the midsummer ceremony - King Keneth of Riz, Queen Nola of Basheba, King

Lordworm of Loungland, Queen Rita of Massive, Princess Anna of Noland, and Prince Bell of Mellington. These were a few of the *haute classe* among the thousand invited who responded favourably to King Bernard's invitation. The others were still feuding with Viz due to several past diplomatic scandals.

The royal invitees were welcomed into the banquet hall by the royal family of Viz. Several traditional delicacies like crayfish with vodka, herring, potatoes, dill sauce, and strawberries and cream were served. Everyone marvelled at the enormous strawberry cake that almost touched the ceiling of the banquet hall, which Maria and her team of cooks had baked. It was coated with brown chocolate dust, white cream, and lingonberries. Every mouth salivated at the sight of it, and she and her team of cooks received praises from several guests.

Non-royal guests were accommodated in tents that were set up outdoors. People ate, drank, and danced happily to the tunes of the traditional folk music, and dancing circles grew bigger and bigger. Just before the midsummer night dance, crowds stood outside the castle in wait of the royal family. Everyone was eager for the appearances of Queen Ursula, Queen Malgory, and King Rowel, who were rarely seen.

King Bruno gave a two-minute opening speech, followed by King Benjamin, who gave the following speech:

> Dear people of Viz, I know everyone is eager for the dance to begin, hence, I'll be brief. Midsummer celebration is a merry event, a time for sharing with family and friends, during which harmony, happiness, and gratitude should be the focus. It is important that you live a life free from stress and worries, and remember to always enjoy it. To enjoy your living, I also created Friday pinky parties.
>
> Life is good. Enjoy it.
>
> You certainly heard about my last feud with King Bruno. This affected me so much, to the point that I couldn't eat or sleep. From this experience, I learned that nothing was worth happiness and that King Bruno, I cared for. I seize this occasion to excuse ourselves for such disroyal behaviour, which isn't exemplary for families

and which almost caused the non-holding of this event. Thanks to King Bernard, this did not happen.

To end my short speech: Enjoy yourselves, and happy midsummer celebration!

The crowd applauded and whistled enthusiastically, although one could not tell if it was because of his apology, his uncharacteristically short speech, or their excitement about the event that was more grandiose than ever this year.

As King Bernard stood up to make his speech, he glanced at King Bruno, who smiled at King Benjamin in appreciation. "Kings Bruno and Benjamin said it all," he said. "I know everyone is eager for the start of the midnight midsummer dance. Happy midsummer to everyone, and let the dance begin!"

Everyone shouted with enthusiasm and started dancing while the royal family and their guests retreated to their various apartments in the castle.

That night, Earl requested an audience with Queen Ursula for the next day.

Chapter 6

Will Queen
Ursula Listen?

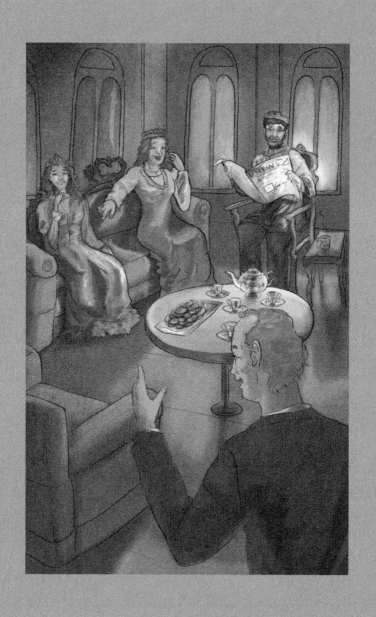

B y midday the next morning, the sun was smiling high in the sky. All the royal guests had left for their homes when Earl rang at Queen Ursula's door.

"Who is here to trouble my old, tired brain?" Queen Ursula teased.

"It's me, your worrisome and faithful friend," Earl responded.

"Come in, worrisome friend," she replied.

Queen Ursula was extremely elegant. She had long legs that accentuated her tall height and gracious walk. Her hard, imperfect facial features were softened by her platinum blonde hair and mysterious green eyes. Her sophisticated demeanour and well-kept appearance concealed the great strength and intelligence which had earned her great admiration during her time of reign.

Earl was invited into the immaculate white room where her husband sat reading on a royal white armchair framed with gold. Queen Malgory had been there much earlier for a warm morning chat with her sister.

"Would you like some ginger cookies and green tea?" Queen Ursula inquired.

"Yes please," he replied.

"Tell me, my friend, what brings you here?" she asked while she served him.

"Your highness, I would like to make known my worries about the future of Viz. I can't condone this situation any longer. Someday, the three kings will turn this kingdom upside down. And Princess Experalda will quickly propel it to that stage sooner than we expect. Her ambitions grow bigger day by day. It will be disastrous if you don't intervene now. I foresee this," he said.

"What have the boys and their sister been up to now?"

"They have been up to the same old stuff, which is getting worse." He then proceeded to explain his concerns about their ruling methods, the latest feud between kings Bruno and Benjamin, and Princess Experalda's ambition to have them fight each other. Queen Ursula observed that he spoke with much ardour. *It must be getting serious*, she thought.

When he finished recounting the events, Queen Ursula said, "I had sworn to myself never to meddle in the boys' ruling. Let them make their own mistakes and learn."

"Your highness, people learn from their mistakes if only they will, but not these three. They are so unaware of the consequences of their actions, which will ruin Viz if nothing is done. We should do everything possible to reorientate their focus, for I am afraid the riches our ancestors worked so hard for shall be squandered and when nothing is left, this will then lead to their exchange of Viz's land resources for gold in order to keep up with their imprudent spending. Subsequently, this will affect people's standard of living, and they will then be miserable from an impoverished lifestyle. And you know what happens to a country when its people are discontent?Another danger lurking is Princess Experalda's zeal to bring them down at any cost. For these reasons, your highness, I implore your intervention for if you don't act, Viz and your sons will be be reduced to ashes."

"Earl, I'm afraid I can't do anything," said Queen Ursula thoughtfully. "If they can't contain greatness and manage it, then they'll be destroyed by it and subjected to a disastrous lifestyle. Then they might learn. Allow them. If it is meant that they be failures, then history will have it that three royal idiots failed in their duties. I inculcated them with good values when they were younger, but if these have been outgrown, what can I do?

"As a child becomes older, he belongs not to you, for though you may have moulded him in good ways, the world will fashion him otherwise. Then it's the child's choice to choose good or bad," Queen Ursula said.

"In a sense, you're right, but I believe that a timely intervention could guide the child back to the right path. No matter the age, a child remains a child," said Earl.

He continued, " Regarding their absurd behaviour, I'm beginning to believe more and more in Manuela's story about Prince Hans. Look at these boys. Basically, at first sight, they seem quiet normal. Bruno loves order and to control everyone, Benjamin likes people, and Bernard enjoys analysing things. Despite this, it seems as though something hinders them from behaving in a rational manner. They're without sense of purpose. As I mentioned earlier, I begin to believe in Manuela's recount of their bewitchment by Hans," Earl said.

"You know I don't believe in sorcery. There is no logic to magic," Queen Ursula said.

"Good heavens! You still haven't changed, Ursula," Queen Malgory chimed in. "For you, any illogic is unreal. Everyone living in Viz and far-off kingdoms has talked about the boys' bewitchment. They say they have been under a curse since their birth. Just look at their behaviours, so weird for kings."

"Let them talk. I still am not convinced about this mumbo-jumbo stuff. The world of magic and bewitchment is simply an illusion," argued Queen Ursula.

"Never underestimate the power of illusion," Earl jumped in. "Let me take you back to the days when the boys were born. Remember how your selfish, evil uncle, Prince Hans Pontus, had undertaken a long journey simply to visit you because he seemed happy about the births of his three nephews? This, despite his non-apology for several years of family feud with your father, King Benedict Pontus, and you.

"Don't you recall how he claimed he enjoyed spending time with your baby boys – which surprised everyone, for it was known that he hated your father for having been ordained king instead of him? You're very much aware how bitter he felt because your grandfather, King Edward II Pontus, had enthroned your father king instead of him. It was also well known that his ill-willed wife, Princess Winona, could not bear him heirs. He was jealous of your father, who had kids but not him. His enthusiasm about your sons made people believe that he might have changed, but this was proved wrong when Manuela's story about him ran across the kingdom.

"I never informed you about this incident because I knew you wouldn't believe it. Manuela recounted that one night, while everyone slept, she awoke to some strange noise coming from the babies' room. Curious about these sounds, she went to check if the boys were all right. As she entered the bedroom, she saw Prince Hans performing some incantations while the babies cried hysterically. He had carried them from their cot, the Dream Sofa, and placed them on the floor. Their foreheads had been stained with some green fluid that dripped from the bottle he held in his hand. When he saw her, he pushed her hard to the side and quickly ran out of the room. After she had cleaned the babies and put them back to sleep on the Dream Sofa, she noticed she had the same green fluid on her arm.

"The next day, she reported the incident to Ingrid and me, and when we sought to get more explanation from Prince Hans, we realized that he had left Viz without notice. A week after his visit, the Dream Sofa disappeared. This was no coincidence. Rumour had it that he was responsible for its disappearance, since it was their cradle. It was claimed that he did so to complete his ritual on the boys, since Manuela's presence had hindered him from finalizing his act. Surprisingly, a while after, Manuela went off her senses and started behaving strange, which had us replace her, unfortunately, with another nanny," Earl concluded.

"I'd never heard this story before," Queen Ursula said. "I had asked myself why you'd employed another nanny when the babies were fond of Manuela, and I often wondered why Uncle Hans left without notice. After his sudden departure, we never heard from him, despite several letters I sent informing him of how his nephews were doing as they grew up. I must admit I was naive there, to think that if a snake wore different shoes, it could walk without being sly.

"All this wickedness from him, for what reason? He had everything: gold, his own property, and unmeasurable riches. Anyway, enough of Uncle Hans. My mind becomes polluted whenever I think of him. However, Manuela's story doesn't change my opinion or belief about the existence of sorcery," Queen Ursula insisted.

"With all due respect, I am pretty convinced that Manuela's story was true," said Earl, "for she displayed the same weird behaviour like the triplets do right now. These strange happenings make me believe that there are good and evil powers that can influence human behaviour.

"If our kings continue to behave this way," he went on, "I'm afraid of what will befall Viz. Let's prevent this while there's still time. I believe finding the Dream Sofa and bringing it back to Viz will reinstate order. Its disappearance might be linked to their strange behaviour – and as such, their destinies – because it was their starting point in life. Ingrid might hint us more on that. I often caught her murmuring stuff about the Dream Sofa, the Bearer, and the Coat, and I thought she was just an old lady going insane," Earl concluded.

"Your arguments have partly convinced me," said Queen Ursula, "though I still don't believe that magic can influence the way people act. I've known you to be a man who served, and still does, with incredible integrity, and I've never regretted having you in my service. For this reason, I'll intervene, since this is your plea. Summon the kings and Ingrid tomorrow for a meeting. We have to solve this situation once and for all," Queen Ursula retorted.

"You honour me, your highness. Your command is an order," Earl exclaimed, his face lighting up.

"Good heavens! This excites me," exclaimed Queen Malgory. "I'm all for this. Let's bring back honour to Viz. Let's bring back our Dream Sofa!"

During the hours that followed, Queen Ursula, Queen Malgory, and Earl brainstormed on how to go about things. The Dream Sofa had been a royal pride. On it had slept several royal descendants, and people even conferred it with divine powers. Its disappearance had shocked every living being in Viz.

Chapter 7

Revelations

The next morning, the triplet kings looked anxious as they wondered why their mother, the retired queen, had summoned them for an urgent meeting.

The presence of Ingrid Wickstrom did not make them feel better, and several thoughts ran across their minds. King Bruno feared that their mother wanted to regain control of the throne. King Benjamin thought he would be blamed for not having been involved sufficiently with the affairs of Viz. King Bernard hoped she had something to reveal.

Tension grew as they waited in the Russian Roulette room. King Benjamin kept wiping thick sweat from his forehead with his flowery handkerchief that he always had on him.

Their mother arrived at exactly 10:30 a.m., accompanied by King Rowel. As they walked into the room, everyone present – the kings, Queen Malgory, Earl Wintor, and Ingrid – all stood up in respect.

She got straight to the point as she sat, saying, "I'm pretty certain you should ask yourselves the purpose for this meeting. Well, word has come to me that this kingdom is going upside down. When you were enthroned as kings, I made an oath never to interfere in your rule, but I also promised myself that if someday you needed help, I would be there. That day has come."

The three kings looked at each other as she said this.

Upside down? What is she up to now? To my best knowledge, our ruling is excellent, thought King Bruno.

Oh, now she'll blame me. Why does she like so much drama? King Benjamin pondered.

No revelations today. Too bad, King Bernard brooded.

"I'm fully aware of what has been going on for years in Viz, and may I say, governing people is similar to having a hen that lays golden eggs. The day you kill that hen, you lose everything. Kings are meant to serve people, to ensure that they have the basic necessities and opportunities to become resourceful and, as such, better citizens. I would have loved to see this with your governance, which unfortunately I don't. This disappoints me, for it would have been preferable that I fail as a leader than watch you fail. I'm sorry to say so, but you've failed in your duties as leaders. This is my reason for being here today.

She continued,"I believe order should be restored where reason has failed. Viz is supposed to go forward, not backwards. Resources have been wasted on unnecessary activities which have transformed your citizens to beggars, and your incessant arguments have dug them more into their unresolved worries, making them frustrated people. Know this: The fate of those you govern depends very much on your actions. In addition, your diplomatic scandals have put Viz in a delicate condition due to reduced allies. I would like this to end."

There she goes. Madame Noble wants the kingdom back, King Bruno thought.

"Act 15 of the kingdom of Viz states this: ' ... though the kings' ordinances are final, in the event of an unresolved disagreement among them, the decisive word lies with the queen.' Forgive me for acting this way. I've no intention of overlooking your authority, but I'm afraid I'll have to apply this measure and ask you to make your rule more efficient. Hence, I propose that the following changes be made: King Bruno will oversee the running of the castle as well as financial matters in close collaboration with kings Benjamin and Bernard, who will approve or disapprove any decision they find unfit. Disapproval will be settled through voting, and the highest count will determine the final decision. If still one of you finds the decision inappropriate, Earl's opinion will be sought, and his remarks will be decisive in resolving the matter.

"King Benjamin will oversee the organization of all events, while King Bernard will be in charge of diplomatic affairs (which will be reinstated) as well as counselling the citizens during audiences. Audiences with royalty and nobles of other kingdoms shall be programmed on Tuesdays as we'd done before. For this, Earl will assist King Bernard in re-establishing friendly relations with kingdoms we have lost as friends. Wednesdays and Fridays shall be scheduled for listening to people issues.

"Audience sessions will be recorded by a secretary and will be reported to kings Bruno and Benjamin to keep them abreast of foreign matters as well as people issues. Earl will support you in your various roles, for I want the kingdom of Viz to be affluent as before.

"Moreover, to ensure that the riches of Viz aren't wasted on futile stuff, I recommend the abolition of weekly events like Games Day, ballroom parties, and Charity Days. To avoid your citizens from alienating themselves to you for this, these events shall only be held once a year, during our birthday.

"Is it okay by you? You all look disheartened. Can I continue?" Queen Ursula inquired.

The three nodded like kids. She went on:

"I also recommend that Charity Day be oriented towards rewarding citizens who have demonstrated acts of outstanding valour and merit that have been of service to our community. This new approach to charity will prevent you from building a city of beggars.

"In light of all that has been said and with view of the fact that you are acting kings of Viz, may I get your consent for these measures to be put into immediate effect? I would be gratified if these rules would be applied as though they were yours," Queen Ursula concluded.

The three kings answered in unison: "We agree."

She then continued, "Good. This makes me happy. Earl, see to it that these measures be implemented as soon as possible.

"Now Ingrid," she continued, "I guess you should be aware of your reason for being here. Just like your late father, your loyalty has been irreproachable, and you have been entrusted with secrets that only a chosen few knew about. Could you reveal to us the mystery of the Multicoloured Coat? Don't forget to let us know about the Dream Sofa and the Bearer. Please, go ahead," Queen Ursula said.

Now we're talking, King Bernard thought, making himself more comfortable on the Victorian sofa.

"My dad, Ingerman Vong Wickstrom, had lots of setbacks in life," Ingrid began. "His first wife passed away too soon, and she bore him a son. Till date, we don't know the whereabouts of this son. Some years later, he remarried my mum, who passed away too, and she bore him another son. To begin life afresh, he took us - Winter Windstorm and I - to Viz. Due to his gift in several languages, he was employed as the librarian of the royal castle's library. His skill enabled him to interpret several books that were translated to Vizmaric [the language spoken in Viz.]. Later on, King Benedict noticed he was trustworthy and promoted him to the position of the Guardian of Ancestral Treasures.

"On his dying bed, my father appointed me as the next Guardian of Ancestral Treasures, since the king had asked that he find someone worthy to take on this role. Before he died, he revealed to me all the secrets. He forbade me to tell anyone, even my brother, Winter, who he had never trusted. I was also given the keys to the room of ancestral treasures as well as the Book of Prophecies and told to keep these carefully as though my life depended on them.

"He told me the Dream Sofa was a cradle of life and that someday, when the Bearer would be found, only he would have the ability to unleash its potential and wear the Multicoloured Coat. He alone would read the Book of Prophecies, which provides insight about the past, the present, and the future," Ingrid told them.

"Is there anyone else who knows about this?" King Bernard inquired.

"Queen Ursula and Winter, who had eavesdropped on my dad's conversation and wanted to know more about it, which I refused to reveal despite his threats."

At Ingrid's response, King Bernard glanced at his mother, whose face stood stone-still. *As I'd suspected, she knows more than she says,* King Bernard thought.

"After my father's death, I hid the keys to the room of ancestral treasures, the Book of Prophecies, and the Multicoloured Coat where no one would find them, for I feared that Winter would do everything in his power to take these from me. My dad had always said that Winter was an ill-intended fellow who would do anything for power. He never liked Winter's friendly tie with Prince Hans.

"Last year, I took out the Multicoloured Coat from its hiding place, as I sensed that the Bearer's time was approaching. We guardians are endowed with special powers to discern changing seasons and interpret time. To have such ability, another guardian should initiate you into this practise, which my dad had done long before he passed away," Ingrid spoke while taking out the Book of Prophecies from the little green bag which hung on her shoulder.

The book's cover was adorned with brown diamonds. At the sight of it, everyone gasped in awe, even Queen Ursula, who had heard of it but never seen it. The light shining from the book was blinding, and mesmerizing sounds came out of it.

"What are these sounds?" King Bernard asked, overwhelmed by all that he had just heard.

"Yes, tell us! We are curious about these sounds," exclaimed King Benjamin, whose eyes were wide open as he stared, impressed by the Book of Prophecies.

"Its pages are blank!" King Bernard exclaimed.

"Unfortunately, I can't interpret these sounds, and neither can I read the blank pages. Only the Bearer is able to do so," Ingrid said.

"Where is he? How can we find him?" King Bruno inquired.

"The only clue I have in identifying him is that he stands on the shoulders of giants. I am pretty certain that very soon, he'll be discovered," Ingrid answered.

Then Queen Ursula interrupted, "Since you sense that his discovery time is drawing closer, we should begin his search, and I would like to confide this mission to the triplets and Earl. The fate of this kingdom lies in your hands, boys. That's enough for today, and tomorrow is another day!" she concluded.

At this, everyone retreated. Ingrid's word kept on resonating in King Bernard's mind. He could hardly go to sleep, for it seemed as though he had heard this phrase before: *He stands on the shoulders of giants, He stands on the shoulders of giants, He stands on the shoulders of giants ...*

The next morning, Princess Gwendoline could tell her mum was irritated from her looks and the way she was dressed: she wore a velvet dress and had her hair loose, not in her usual bun.

"Mum, why are you angry? Has someone offended you?" she inquired.

"My sweet doll, I'm not mad at you. It's Grandma with whom I have scores to settle," Princess Experalda said.

"Grandma? Why?" Princess Gwendoline inquired.

"I'll inform you later. I have to hurry now," Princess Experalda said and left for her mother's residence. Princess Gwendoline descended downstairs to the main dining room for breakfast, where her favourite grand-aunt and uncles sat having theirs too.

"Mother, I wasn't convened for yesterday's meeting. Why?" Princess Experalda asked angrily.

"It was none of your concern. Your presence wasn't needed," Queen Ursula said.

"May I ask why? You always exclude me from important matters," Princess Experalda said as tears welled up in her eyes.

"I did so because your brothers are the rulers of Viz, not you. Besides, your intention isn't always right. Why should you be involved? If you want to be involved in the matters of Viz, talk to your brothers, not me. I'm simply a retired queen."

"Then let me be the active queen," Princess Experalda said sarcastically.

"I'm afraid only the kings can do that. I don't have the authority," Queen Ursula answered.

"But you did have it yesterday when you convened the meeting and made some changes. Benjamin recounted to me all what happened when I asked him where they'd been that evening. I demand that you use the acts and appoint me king too."

"No, I can't do that. By the way, why do you get me up from sleep at such an early hour? It's only 7:45 a.m., and you know very well that my sleep lasts till nine o'clock. Could you leave now? I've got some sleep to catch," Queen Ursula said.

"Injustice! Unjust. Mother, you are so unfair to me. You will regret this. Everyone keeps ignoring me, whereas I'm smarter than my brothers. You'll regret this. Wait and see!" Princess Experalda banged the front door as she left.

Yes indeed, you are smarter, but you lack a people's heart, Queen Ursula murmured to herself while staring at the door which had just been slammed.

After breakfast, Princess Gwendoline followed her grand-aunt, Queen Malgory, to the guest apartments. As they came to Queen Malgory's room, Princess Gwendoline asked lots of questions, as all little girls do: "What is this, Grand-Aunt Malgory?"

"Oh that! It's my red lipstick," Queen Malgory replied.

"Red lipstick? What's it used for? Is there an orange lipstick too?" Princess Gwendoline asked.

"Women use lipsticks to colour their lips to make them look more beautiful, and yes, there is also orange lipstick, and other lipsticks of several colours," Queen Malgory replied.

"Beautiful, but you don't need that, you're already so pretty. Can I use it too? I'm a woman, you know? But why do you need red lips for? Your lips are pink," Princess Gwendoline said.

"Unfortunately, lipsticks are only for grown-ups. Let's say I prefer to change lip colour from time to time," she answered.

"Me too! I would like to change my lips to orange. Could I have an orange lipstick?" Princess Gwendoline said.

"But your lips are perfect, my dear," Queen Malgory replied.

"Not as perfect as Leslie's. We're in the same class, and she has these very green beautiful eyes and orange lips. Everyone adores her, including the teachers," Princess Gwendoline said.

"My darling, every little girl is beautiful in a unique way, because they come from roses. You are beautiful too and the most intelligent little girl in Viz," Queen Malgory said. Princess Gwendoline smiled when she said so.

"Will I wear make-up when I'm grown?" inquired Gwendoline

"Yes, if you desire," Queen Malgory replied.

Princess Gwendoline's face radiated as she smiled in joy that someday she will grow up and wear make-up too. She really liked her grand-aunt because the woman treated her like an adult and never like a child, the same way her uncles Bruno and Bernard did.

Queen Malgory spent one more week in Viz before she travelled back to Gothen. She wished them good luck in their quest for the Bearer as her chariot disappeared into the thin air of that cold Sunday morning.

Chapter 8
Game Zone

The outside of the castle had been transformed into a gigantic playing field. There was a contest going on, and several areas had been demarcated for the games, where thousand of participants would test their abilities in hope of being the Bearer.

On the north side of the castle, Princess Experalda stood watching from afar eager faces impatiently waiting for the contest to begin. *As usual, I've not been involved in this. I will teach them a lesson,* she reflected vengefully.

Meanwhile, prior to this contest, King Bernard carried out extensive research on the Bearer. He looked for every clue he could get. He reread all the books in the library - for Ingrid's words "He stands on the shoulders of giants" sounded familiar. He also asked Ingrid for any other information he could obtain, but she was not very talkative, and it seemed as though his efforts were in vain as he sought useful information from her.

His brothers and everyone else in the castle were also involved in this quest. They sought out information from any source as well as their acquaintances. In fact, the whole of Viz had been involved, as people asked their neighbours and friends if they knew anything about the Bearer. Any helpful information was reported to the castle. Even SpyBrow participated, sharing with King Bernard the discussions he had collected around town, for the Bearer was now the talk of the whole city and a bedtime story for kids.

King Bernard had been most keen on finding the Bearer, and it had seemed like ages. One weary afternoon, when it felt like his quest led to no where, though he sensed the answer was somewhere, he insisted on having the keys to the Ancestral Treasure Room, but Ingrid, stubborn as a mule, would not let him. He thought she had made guarding the treasures an obsession rather than a duty, and he bluntly told her this. In defence, she argued that she would be obsessed until the Bearer was found. Pissed off, she was told that might happen only when she dozed in her grave. Finally, after long discourse hours, she handed him the keys to the treasure room - but stood outside in wait while he went in.

As he entered the room of ancestral treasures, King Bernard almost choked from the dust that had accumulated, which made him wonder what sort of cleaning Ingrid had been carrying out with her staff throughout the years. In her eighties, she had grown so frail from the years of intense responsibility that she could no longer be as meticulous as before in her supervisory role – she would not let anyone but herself do the job.

Wandering through the various corridors that harboured statues, amour, gold, and lots of goods of great worth, King Bernard left no object untouched, hoping to get clues that could help him. After a while, he came across a grey door faded with age. He opened it and was disappointed as he entered a dark room in which several old coats hung on the walls. Dismayed at this sight, he almost cried out of anguish – but then he noticed in the left corner of the room a brown box carelessly placed on the floor, covered with cobwebs.

By this time, his curiosity was at its peak. He struggled to open the box and his countenance brightened when he saw what was in it: an English novel dating from the third century. Immediately, he remembered that he had read it when he was six; at that time, it was among the books found in the library. Someone had hidden it here – *Ingrid, of course*, he thought. As he flipped through the pages, it all became so clear where the words which had sounded so familiar originated from. Elated was he when he found this on page nineteen: "He Stood on the Shoulders of Giants." There were also some handwritten notes in the box, which he proceeded to quickly read. The letter had the signature of his great-great-grandfather, King Edward I Pontus, and it was addressed to King Edward II Pontus, his only son:

Dear beloved son,

My rule will soon come to an end, and I am proud to have had you as a son. You loyally stood by me when the night was darkest. Never a day did you oppose me in counsel, even when your opinion was different from mine, and thereafter, circumstances had sometimes proved me wrong. You have demonstrated kingship qualities and an unsurpassed maturity which merits that you be ordained king, and I shall enthrone you the soonest, for my health is failing me and I have only a few more years ahead of me. I am eager to experience your reign because I am convinced it will be full of might, and I desire to see your feats with my very own eyes, rather than hear about them from the depths of the grave.

In addition, I would like to entrust you with a long-kept family secret: the Multicoloured Coat which someday will be worn by the Bearer. Thousands of generations have awaited his discovery to no avail, and it has been said of him that he stands on the shoulders of giants and has the compassion of a god. His sight is piercing like the eagle's and more other characteristics define him. Decoding the secrets of the Ancestral Treasure Room would lead to him. I hoped I would witness his existence during my reign, but this has not been. Hopefully, you will be fortunate to do so. If not, pass this secret on to someone trustworthy. There are several mysteries still to be unveiled about the Multicoloured Coat and the Bearer, which I will reveal later upon your return from your victorious Battle of Rain. I just wanted to pour my heart out to you in case you do not find me alive. In hope of seeing you, King Edward I Pontus.

King Bernard carefully folded the letter into the box as well as the novel titled *The Mid-Night Lullaby*, which he took along with him for a reread with Ingrid's approval. Puzzled by the room's mystery, he returned to the Ancestral Treasure Room forty times with Ingrid's accord in hope of unveiling its secrets, though to no avail.On the brink of despair, he devised a scheme to organize games meant to discover the Bearer. With the information he had at hand, his brothers and he then elaborated quizzes and tests as tools that would lead to the Bearer.

The castle now looked like a vast playground, or more like a buzzing beehive. Contestants scurried around as they attempted the various tests under the watchful eyes of the Game Masters who stood around every corner to rate and rank the various performances. Nobody wanted to be scored low, and all strived to be number one. Unfortunately, that was not the fate of everyone.

The crowd watched enthusiastically and laughed as contestants fell from the thin rope placed at the starting point of contest area A. In this section, the rope had been raised on two wooden poles and was meant to disqualify and reduce the number of participants who came from the north, the south, the east, and the west of the kingdom. All the competitors began by climbing the pole from one end and walking over the thin rope to the other end of the pole with raised hands and without falling. Agility, a distinctive quality of the Bearer, was required to pass this test.

Among the contestants was Dumbbell, and people were surprised that he made it through the starting point, for he was an old drunkard who told jokes and was good at riddles. He was the famous fool of Viz.

After the rope phase, participants were challenged with games aimed at testing intelligence, strength, compassion, courage, ego, and wisdom. Contestants also entered obscure holes and crawled through them to the other end of the game zone and then climbed slippery walls. The games were tough; some appeared to be easy, but all had been designed to be tricky, for it was said that the Bearer would overcome any obstacle.

Questions on metric horsepower were asked, challenges on using the five senses were set, mind-teasing quizzes were spelled out, and queries meant to depict wisdom were the order of the day. The masterminds behind these games, the triplet kings, keenly observed from the front balcony as they watched contestants qualify from one stage to the next and hoped that one of them was the Bearer.

After several hours of questing, striving, and puzzling, five participants made it to the final phase. The last test was to tame a lion enclosed in a cage. This was a team task which required that the final contestants divide themselves in two groups. They were asked to select their teammates, but no one wanted to be on the same team as Dumbbell, who to everyone's amazement had made it to the final five. Dumbbell's reputation as a good-for-nothing person ran across kingdoms.

The judges took a long pause to deliberate on the fact that Dumbbell was the only person in his group while the other team was made up of four members. As they deliberated, they decided to allow fate to have its way.

The two groups were provided with tools to be used in taming the lion, among which were a chair, an armour, a whip, a big lump of meat, a torch, many sharp pins, a spear, and several bows and arrows. Dumbbell, for being alone in his group, was given the privilege of choosing first, and he choose a chair, a whip, a torch, and the lump of meat. The other four mocked his choice, which they deemed stupid, for he had taken what none of them wanted. The crowd laughed at him too.

The team of four was then asked to begin their attempt. At this, they entered the cage, with the spear bearer heading, one step at a time, towards the lion, armoured from head to toe. He was cautiously followed by two teammates whose heartbeats could be heard from a distance, one on his left and the other on his right, both of whom directed their arrows at the lion. The fourth guy walked behind them holding the pins in his hands, and as he received a signal from those ahead of him, he made a quick run ahead and pinned the pins on the ground in front of the lion. These were meant to prevent the lion from pouncing at them, but instead, it enraged the creature even more. The lion roared and stood defiantly on its legs as it started threateningly at them.

At this, the spear guy screamed as he, in panic, sought refuge behind the arrow bearers. It had the lion pounce at them as they scurried to safety out of the cage. Fortunately, they made their way out in time. Some onlookers reacted with horror while others laughed incessantly.

When the lion had calmed down, Dumbbell was ushered in. He tied the torch around his head and lit it as he threw the lump of meat in front of the lion. He then placed the chair close to where the lion lay eating. After the animal had finished its meal, he encircled it. The moving torch distracted the lion from pouncing, for it was confused on what or who to attack. The meat had also weakened it, yet despite this, it struggled to approach Dumbbell, who lashed the whip at it to set the space between them. After several attempts by the lion to attack, it finally surrendered.

At this, Dumbbell placed the cord round his neck, took it to the smaller cage, and locked it. Proud of this feat, he raised his hands up in victory as the crowd applauded and cheered out loud.

A while after, Dumbbell stood on the podium that had been raised for the winner, grinning from ear to ear as he awaited the gold-medal reward which was to be handed to him by the kings. As he received this prize, the latter congratulated him, and Ingrid was asked to bring along the Multicoloured Coat for him to wear. Given the exploit he had just accomplished, it was certain that he was the Bearer.

Before the coat was handed to him, however, Dumbbell exclaimed fervently, "Me not, me not the Bearer, my lords. Let me not defile it by having it on me. It won't fit. Though I may have won the contest, I am not the Bearer."

As he spoke these words, everything became dead. Frozen, King Benjamin gasped for air while King Bruno, boiled at a temperature of 100°C, insisted that Dumbbell wear the coat, for he only believed what he saw.

"As you please, my lord," Dumbbell replied. "I will try on the coat, but I still insist on not being the Bearer." Dumbbell put on the Multicoloured Coat, and as he had said, it did not fit. It was way too small.

At the sight of this, King Bernard's face lost all colour. He had never been so pale. "What shall we do now that Dumbbell is not the Bearer? From my calculations, the probability was very high for us to discover the Bearer during these games. I don't know what to do now," he said, unaware that he spoke his thoughts out loud to be heard by everyone.

Princess Experalda thundered an excruciating laugh, which echoed all over the place as she turned towards her mother who stood by her. "In life, those who walk alone fall alone," she crowed. "If you'd involved me in this plan, I would have told you that destiny is never brought to reality through mathematical assumptions but only through revelations of hidden history facts. Hahahahaha! Hahahahaha! Hahahahaha! Idioooooooots! Hahahahaha! Your darling boys have done it once again."

At her words, Dumbbell fervently spoke, "Excuse me, my lady, may I pursue with what I've to say?"

"Of course, good-for-nothing winner, you may talk," Princess Experalda said, enjoying the fact that her brothers had made fools of themselves before everyone through the unrealistic organization of this contest.

"It was announced that the kings were in search of the Bearer, I tried so hard to convince whoever could listen that I knew where the Bearer lived, but no one paid attention to the words of an old drunkard who had nothing to show for in life but riddles. In an attempt to make myself heard, I decided to participate in this contest, with hopes that if I won, then all ears would listen to me."

"That's impossible," King Bruno declared in agitation. "You can't know about the Bearer. It's impossible. How could that be? If you know about him, why didn't you bring him along?"

"Pardon my insistence, my lord. I know who the Bearer is, and I think he lives east from here, deep in the woods. I could take you there."

"You think or you are certain about where he lives? Why didn't you make him participate in the games if what you're saying is true?" King Bruno's face reddened as he spoke.

"Please, my lord, forgive my inconsistent words. I know where he lives."

"Then why didn't you bring him to us if that's the case?" King Bruno continued angrily.

"Time was not on my side, my lord. I had word about this contest one week before it began, and it takes three weeks travelling by horse to the Bearer," Dumbbell said.

"Why hadn't you reported to the castle on this, as most people do when they find out useful information about the Bearer?" King Bruno asked.

"I didn't know we were to report on any news about the Bearer. I'm sorry for this, but I did my best to tell people about my knowledge of him. Unfortunately, they didn't listen."

"If you hadn't made it to the winning position, how would you have voiced out your knowledge about the Bearer?" King Benjamin asked.

"If I'd failed the games, I would have caused a commotion that would have taken me before you, my lords, and then I would have revealed about the Bearer," Dumbbell replied.

"If you know the Bearer, when did you last see him, and how can you ascertain that indeed he is the Bearer?" continued King Bruno.

"A year ago, while I wandered about the counties of Viz as I usually do, I came across a little cottage after weeks of travelling by foot.

Exhausted, I met this family whom I asked for food and water before continuing my journey. I was warmly welcomed and offered some shelter until I regained my strength. During my stay at their place, I noticed strange happenings beyond my understanding. There was this unique young man who captivated my attention. Words cannot explain what I experienced. I just knew he was the Bearer," Dumbbell said.

"And what were these strange signs? Drunkard hallucinations?" interrupted Princess Experalda. "Stop this gibberish. You of all people, drunk all year long, who probably knows not how to spell his name, can discern signs which identify the Bearer? Nothing proves that you're truthful."

"My lady, you may be right. Nothing shows that what I say is true, but though a man be drunk, he will at least know how to say his name. Words cannot explain what I saw in that family, and though I drown my miseries in wine, I know what I saw," Dumbbell explained.

"Enough of this!" Queen Ursula exclaimed. "We'll finish what we began. I recommend that Dumbbell and a group of fellows go to the Bearer's home as soon as possible and bring him here."

"Great idea, Mum. I will be part of this group. Dumbbell, I look forward to experiencing the strange things you saw at the Bearer's home," King Bernard exclaimed as colour returned to his face.

"I will be part of this journey too," exclaimed King Benjamin, clapping his hands excitedly. "It would be awesome to travel and meet new people along the way," he said, one hand placed on his forehead and the other on his waist.

Then King Bruno instructed, "So shall it be. You guys will be part of this journey, though I would have preferred that Dumbbell bring this young man to us. Perhaps the presence of two kings shall be more credible and will convince the Bearer to follow the group to Viz. Kings Benjamin and Bernard should make arrangements for this journey. Earl will accompany you too. Dumbbell, if you dare return without the Bearer, severe sanctions await you in Viz. I know you wouldn't want Winter Wickstrom's fate to befall you," King Bruno concluded.

That said, the contest ended. The staff started dismantling the constructed game site while the crowd approached Dumbbell, praising his victory at the games and inquiring as to his certainty about the Bearer.

That evening, Dumbbell was the talk of the town.

Chapter 9

The Journey

At four o'clock the next morning, the journey in quest of the Bearer began. To avoid being delayed by the commotion of a waking town as well as the scorching sun, the travellers left very early.

Merry chants were heard inside the carriage as it drove like lightning towards the east and the travelling companions – King Benjamin, King Bernard, Earl, Dumbbell, and Dorland (a servant in charge of food provisions) – sang their lungs out. Two knights rode on horses, one in front the carriage dressed in white armour and the other one behind it in black armour. SpyBrow flew along behind the carriage, curious to see how things would turn out (with Bernard's knowledge).

"What goes down but never comes up?" Dumbbell started his riddles.

"Sun rays," King Benjamin guessed.

"Try again."

"Rain," King Benjamin rephrased.

"Correct," Dumbbell said. "What occurs once in a minute, twice in a moment, and never in one thousand years?"

"Hmm, what occurs once in a minute, twice ..." King Benjamin tried to figure the answer as he rephrased the question under his breath.

"Letter M," King Bernard chimed in.

"Exactly," Dumbbell confirmed. "Take away my first letter, and I still sound the same. Take away my last letter, I still sound the same. Even take away my letter in the middle, I still sound the same. I am a five-letter word," Dumbbell went on, as kings Benjamin and Bernard tried hard to guess which word it was.

"We give up," the kings said.

"Empty," Dumbbell answered.

"May we have some silence, please? Others are trying to get some sleep here. The whole day, you've been incessant with your riddles. We need a break, Dumbbell," Earl jumped in, tired of all the noise.

Dumbbell laughed and threw back at him jokingly, "It ain't for nothing that I'm called the master of riddles."

"Oho! May I ask you, what's the contrary of noise? Silence. We need that now, master of riddles," Earl responded, displeased this time.

At this, everyone became quiet ... for a short while.

"Let me recount my adventures in Greece. It all started when ..." Dumbbell spoke, pretending as though Earl had said nothing.

"Silence signifies *silence*, Dumbbell!" Earl exclaimed, really irritated this time. It surprised and amused everyone to see Earl differ from his usual diplomatic self.

"Yes, but you meant my silence on riddles, not storytelling," Dumbbell teased him.

Tired of this argument, Earl said nothing, folded his arms, looked the other way, and thought to himself, *No need to quarrel with fools, they never understand.*

This made King Benjamin laugh out loud. "Peace be with you, now we will keep quiet, and from time to time we can talk."

Despite these words from King Benjamin, Dumbbell could not stop talking, and his voice echoed out of the carriage. He was endless with his riddles, to King Benjamin's amazement and King Bernard's amusement at his stubbornness. Dumbbell also recounted his travel adventures in various countries and phrased countless jokes that annoyed Earl Wintor, who ignored his rattling sounds and contemplated instead on the serenity of the woods, livened by insects that sang praises to the god of trees.

Five days they had travelled, for what had seemed like centuries. Their bones grew weary from the bumps and potholes on the ride.

"Once upon a time, ten travellers undertook a journey to a fantasy world where there were time elements to be discovered. One of these travellers was ... aieeeeeeeeeeeeee yayaya uuuyuuuuuuuiiiiiii!" Dumbbell had started another fairy tale but out of the blue was interrupted by a sharp bump that knocked off the wheel of the carriage, sending it somersaulting into the air before landing flat on three legs. Screams heightened inside the damaged carriage, and bodies ached even more.

As confused passengers struggled their way out, King Bernard asked Springbell, the carriage driver, "What happened?"

"I mistakenly hit a big stone on the side while making a U-turn. I didn't see it, and one of the wheels was pulled out," Springbell answered.

"Is everybody fine?" King Benjamin asked.

"Yes, we're all doing fine, and none of us is hurt," a chorus of voices answered.

"Thank heavens," King Bernard exclaimed.

Minutes turned to hours as Springbell, assisted by the two knights, struggled to repair the damaged carriage and fix the wheel back to its original position. After hours of struggle, he said, "We can't fix this, my lords. Should we send for help?"

"No. We'll continue by foot and leave the horses here to graze. Nothing should slow us down," King Bernard said.

As drained blood rushed on his right head side, King Benjamin's voice was vehement, "Are you out of your senses? Leave these horses here? What if they are stolen? Why can't we simply ride on their backs? Three or two persons per horse, that sounds reasonable to me. Trekking will slow us down."

"One horse is injured, and we've only two left. Don't forget we're eight in number to mount two horses which is practically impossible, and with your idea, how shall we carry our provisions? We'll be slow no matter the means by which we choose to go, and I find no issue with the horses remaining here in the wild. We've too many in Viz," King Bernard said.

"You're the c-r-a-z-i-e-s-t of my brothers. I thought Bruno was, but you ..." King Benjamin shook his head. "Dumbbell, you've travelled here before. How many days had we ahead before arriving at our destination?"

"Sixteen more days," Dumbbell answered.

"Do you hear that? On horseback we still had sixteen days left, and going on foot might take a month!" King Benjamin almost cried as he spoke.

"Of course, and sitting here doing nothing will take an eternity. We'd better start walking. If Dumbbell survived this walk last year, so can we, and now we'll have to apply Bruno's Thursday Games Day survival skills. You never liked it," King Bernard said as he moved ahead, forcing the others to follow.

"No, I won't walk in these frightful, dark woods. What do you want to accomplish, a trekking feat? Go without me," King Benjamin shouted in irritation.

"Fine, then you'll have to return to Viz and tell them we continued on foot. You could go along with Springbell and one knight and seek help on our behalf. Remember, it'll take five days before reaching Viz," suggested King Bernard.

"No way. I don't want Bruno to think that I'm a fearful freak. I'll go with you, but let Springbell, two knights, and Dorland return for help with a horse while we ride on two carrying a few provisions on our backs," King Benjamin said.

"Don't make me laugh. You, Benjamin, carry a load on your back? You'll complain after a second." King Bernard said and then went on, "Okay, we shall send one knight to Viz to inform the others of our circumstance, but then we the remaining seven shall walk. I won't return to Viz without the Bearer. Never a day. Just imagine Experalda's unconcealed scorn if we fail."

That said, the knight dressed in black armour was given some food rations and sent to seek help in Viz while the rest of the group continued on foot, and two horses (inclusive of the injured one) were released into the wild.

Thereafter, they travelled for six days when, after several hours of walking, King Benjamin's numb legs slowed down as he screeched:

"Please let's stop, we're not in a marathon. What is there for lunch, Dorland?" King Benjamin asked.

"Only two tins of pickled herring are left and one bottle of water," Dorland answered, his face downcast.

"Mamma mia! How come? Have we been eating so much? I had only planned for food supply for three weeks, and we've been travelling for almost eleven days and still have nineteen more days to go. Let's hope help arrives on time," King Benjamin exclaimed in alarm. "OMG! Who brought me here? I hope I won't die of hunger in these woods."

"Cheer up," King Bernard said. "This is a lifetime experience. We shall share one tin for lunch and the other for super. Tomorrow is another day. We will eat fruits from trees as we walk along and refill our bottles with water from any water source."

The following day was not easy at all. Their food and water reserve had finished, and none of these could be found in the thick, dark forest.

The travellers eventually found some wild berries in a thick green bush located eastwards, and though they ate, it was not to their satisfaction. Exhausted and thirsty, some of them complained, especially King Benjamin.

"I will help you search for food and water. Follow me!" SpyBrow tweeted as he sprang out of nowhere.

No one said a word. They just gazed at him in awe.

"Don't look at me like that. You guys are a pitiful sight. Just follow me," SpyBrow continued.

"Heeeeyyy! Am I hallucinating? This is not possible. Do birds talk now? Dehydration is not good. We need water, King Bernard," Dumbbell exclaimed in disbelief.

The others stood paralyzed on their feet, shocked at what they had just witnessed.

"I said, don't stare at me like that!" SpyBrow tweeted as his wings flapped stronger.

King Bernard laughed and proudly said, "No, you're not hallucinating. Let me present to you SpyBrow, my friend."

"What? He even has a name?" they all exclaimed at the same moment.

"*Hello!*", SpyBrow teased.

"Bernard, I thought this Spy thing you spoke so much of was a joke!" King Benjamin said as he recovered from his trance." Earlier this morning, you mentioned something about SpyBrow to Bruno but I was too preoccupied with the journey to listen. How can he speak? Some parrots do mimic words after they've been taught by humans, but not other birds. How did he learn to talk? So your stories about SpyBrow were true," King Benjamin voiced out loud.

"I don't know how. He spoke to me the first time I met him," said King Bernard. "That was three years back, when I noticed that each time I lay in the garden under the birch tree, a peculiar bird perched on it and stared at me. One day I approached and tried to touch him, and to my surprise, he didn't fly away like other birds. This was funny to me, and I said, 'Brave bird, won't you go away?' 'Oh no, I won't,' he had then replied and introduced himself as SpyBrow, a bird from the Ashung Forest in Africa. I was shocked then when he spoke as you are right now. From there on, we became friends."

"Where did you say he came from?" King Benjamin asked in a relaxed tone.

"The Ashung Forest in Africa. Birds of his kind once populated that area, but due to deforestation, they're now extinct. In search of greener pastures, Spy found his way to Viz, the land of trees and sun," King Bernard answered.

"Enough about me. Let's go," SpyBrow tweeted once again.

At this, they followed the bird along a southern route. After a short while, they were led to an area that resembled an orchard, with a river flowing by the trees. This garden-like place had apples, pomegranates, strawberries, berries, and mushrooms.

Everyone cheered at this pleasant view, and they all thanked SpyBrow and quickly ran to fill their grumbling stomachs. They ate and drank to their satisfaction. Too tired to pursue their journey, they slept, almost forgetting themselves and their long route ahead. After two hours of restful sleep, they took reserves and retraced their steps eastwards.

"Follow me, we were south, now let's return east," SpyBrow said. In admiration, they followed him, more astonished than before and wondering if this was real.

There was no sign of life in the hilly landscape except for the lonely trees that surrounded them in a mocking manner and the scorching sun that reminded them of their lost quest. They felt lost in an immense world.

Thirty-one days had gone by, and Dumbbell was in low spirits. That morning, he kept recollecting his childhood memories: his mother had passed away when he was five, his depressed father had taken him to missionary care and then had left. At seventeen, he had tried to get in touch with his father, to no avail. He heard rumours that he worked in a far-off land.

King Bernard listened keenly as Dumbbell spoke, while the others were too engrossed in their travel misery.

As they entered deeper into the thick forest, the hopelessness of their venture became more evident. *We are lost!* Earl thought. *It was a hopeless cause from the onset. Why did we listen to this foolish riddler?*

"My lords," Earl said, "may I request a break, please? I would be most elated if I was granted some time to ease myself." He directed himself into the woods in search of a discreet and convenient place – and then suddenly, he cried out for the others to come.

Alarmed, they quickly ran to his rescue.

"What is it?" King Bernard inquired as he appeared before Earl, surprised at the man's delirious attitude, which was uncommon for him.

"See? Look!" Earl pointed ahead of him. "There's a settlement, a house, a cottage. We're not alone, we're not alone, there are people living in these woods!" he exclaimed enthusiastically.

The others, who had been running behind Bernard, joined them and stared in the direction Earl pointed towards. Indeed, there was a red little cottage with a chimney from which smoke was expelled.

"Hallelujah, hallelujah! We've arrived. Certainly, this is the place, although during my last trip, I'd taken a different path to the cottage," Dumbbell gladly shouted.

Re-energized, they all ran downhill towards the little red cottage.

Chapter 10

Who Is He?

The little red cottage had a vast field adorned with horses that grazed in an enclosed fence. Their stomachs churned as the smell of cheese gracefully swept the air while they drew closer to the house.

The travellers were about to knock on the white wooden door when a male voice spoke from inside: "Come in please."

As they entered the small living room, they were received by an elderly-looking blind man who sat by the lamp that lit the room. He looked like he had been contemplating.

"Welcome to our home, dear travellers. I was expecting your visit today. Anna, would you roast the fattest lamb for our guests?" he said while the kings and their companions gazed at each other, bewildered by what they had just heard.

"Please have a seat." The old man pointed towards two sofas that faced his brown armchair. They were most amazed by this gesture, for he knew exactly where each stood.

A short while after, an old lady in her seventies, Anna, walked into the living room and cheerfully greeted the travellers as the old man introduced the guests. "These are the visitors we had long awaited," he said. "My lords and distinguished guests, I am called Eyon Nordmark, and you are most welcome to our dwelling. Please be our guests for as long as you want. Dumbbell, it is nice seeing you once again. How do you do?"

"How do you do, Eyon? As for me, I'm fine!" Dumbbell said.

"Wonderful! You know, this morning, I told my wife that we would have important guests today." As he spoke, the visitors felt comfortable in the cosy little room.

King Benjamin said, "We're really astonished about your knowing of our coming. How come?"

"Lord Benjamin, when you see butterflies, summer is around the corner. I've been endowed with the gift of vision. I see and foretell the future. I'm the Guide," Eyon said.

At his words (impressed that he also knew Benjamin's name),the travellers exchanged puzzled glances.

"Hadn't I told you that once you got here, you would experience stuff beyond your comprehension?" Dumbbell said, excited that no one would doubt him anymore.

Impressed by what Eyon had said, the kings were curious about his gift and asked a lot of questions. Their discussion lasted for almost three hours, and then Anna served some food in the dining room. For lunch there was a whole roasted lamb with boiled potatoes, hot beef soup, and lettuce salad seasoned with carrots, cucumbers, and tomatoes. A creamy vanilla-chocolate cake was also on the menu, alongside some freshly pressed cranberry juice. They all salivated at the sight of the food, for during their many days of travel, they had not had such a copious meal.

"My lords, please have the honour," Eyon said.

Elated beyond words, the seven travellers served themselves without hesitation. Around the table, there was much merriment.

As they ate dessert, Eyon commented, "I know you have come for the Bearer."

On hearing this, Earl almost choked as he swallowed a bite of cake. Dumbbell, who sat close to him, gave him a strong tap on the back and then handed him a glass of water.

"True, we're here for the Bearer. Does he really exist? How did you know this?" King Bernard inquired.

"His existence has long been foretold, and certainly he does. As I said earlier, I'm the Bearer's Guide, and my gift enables me to see into the past, present, and future. My purpose is to lead the Bearer in the right direction until the appointed time," Eyon said.

"Then if he really exists, where is he? Shouldn't he be here with you?" King Benjamin asked.

"Yes, where is he?" King Bernard inquired, hoping this was not some scam.

"He is out in the fields and will be home by five o'clock," Eyon replied. At his words, those present heaved a sigh of relief, for they had had a subconscious belief that the story about the Bearer was a myth. *Dumbbell was right after all!* everyone thought.

"So, we've two more hours to wait for the Bearer. By the way, if my geography skills are good, I think this is Orebra, isn't it? It is so far from the castle," King Benjamin asked.

"Exactly, the county of Orebra, where the strong and wise dwell," Eyon said.

After lunch, they had cinnamon tea and were later showed around the cottage. The landscape in Orebra was amazing, and the neighbouring houses in view sloped down the valley.

At five o'clock, they went indoors for supper and ate toasted bread with ham. While their discussion was at its peak, a young man entered the living room. He carried a basket full of fruits which he placed by the corner, and then he kissed Anna on the forehead before directing himself to the dining room where the group sat. They were all enchanted by this green-eyed, strong-looking handsome figure moving towards them. His shoulder-length hair floated as he walked.

"Is this the Bearer?" King Benjamin asked.

"No, this is my grandson Mikael Nordmark," Eyon replied. He was about to ask a question of Mikael when he was interrupted by the entrance of a twelve-year-old young fellow.

The boy's countenance was magnetic, and such an aura radiated from him. His olive-green eyes were mysteriously tantalizing. His long, deep, dark hair – wrapped in a bun and tied in between by several dark ribbons – was a good contrast against his white, polished skin.

As he moved towards them with assurance, golden hues emanated from him. King Bernard could not help but think, "*He stands on the shoulder of giants, sits in the counsel of the wise, has the bravery of a lion and the heart of a child. Only he has insights to the prophecies. ... His hair cannot be touched for it is strength.*" Unable to withhold his excitement, he said, "Is he the Bearer?"

"Yes he is," Eyon replied proudly. "My other grandson, Nathanael Nordmark."

Dumbbell was right. There was something unique about this young man whose appearance conveyed dignity. It could be felt that this little boy had unexplainable inner strength. They were all captivated by his person.

"Nathanael, the time is here. Meet our long-awaited guests," Eyon said.

Nathanael moved towards them and bowed before the kings and the guests. Everyone laughed, for he revered them in a funny way.

"Welcome, my lords, we're most honoured by your presence," Nathanael said.

"Oh no, young man, we're rather honoured to meet you," King Benjamin said, and then asked, "Eyon, what did you mean by 'the time is here'?"

"From childhood, Nathanael knew he was the Bearer and that some day he would meet his destiny. He grew under my strict mentorship, following the disappearance of his parents in a shipwreck when Mikael was seven and he two. His parents had knowledge of the fact that he was the Bearer. At six months, this peculiar baby could interpret his dreams and foretell the future. Before his birth, I'd had numerous visions of him and who he was to become.

"'When the time is here, at the appointed moment for you to fulfill your destiny, you'll wear it', I used to say whenever Nathanael eagerly recounted how he saw himself in dreams, wearing the Multicoloured Coat.I told him to direct his zeal on nurturing his gift instead," Eyon explained.

Back in the castle of Viz, King Bruno restlessly paced about the lifeless room atmosphere, worried that his brothers had been gone for six weeks. If things had gone as planned, they would have been home by now.

The knight in the black armour had returned and reported what had happened in the woods. Immediately, help was sent, which turned out to be several days of searching and ended up with no trace of the travellers. Rumour then spread of their disappearance, and the whole kingdom of Viz was troubled because their kings were missing. To dramatize this incidence and make themselves important, some search team members invented stories that were amplified as gossip and went about like a wild bushfire.

Hope they're safe and sound, King Bruno thought.

"Still no news about the travellers?" Queen Ursula asked, her eyes reflecting gloom.

"No, no news still," King Bruno responded.

"I had warned about relying on the words of that old drunkard, Dumbbell, but no one listened," snapped Princess Experalda. "Now everyone is in *worryland*. Not me, though. I believe people should live by the consequences of their actions, and I don't pity those two stupid kings who acted upon their emotions."

"Enough, Experalda! We don't need lessons now," Queen Ursula said.

"This reminds me that Bernard was supposed to send his bird, SpyBrow, ahead of them in case the Bearer was found, and there hasn't been any bird sign yet," King Bruno said.

"Ha! Hope they're still alive," Princess Experalda exclaimed. "Who believes in fairy bird tales, by the way? Not me. Bruno, I can't believe this. Are you aware of how desperate you've become? To the point of believing that SpyBrow story."

"Good heavens, Experalda! You're mean. Let's be positive and keep hoping that everything is fine with them. Who knows, the bird could still be on his way to Viz," Queen Malgory said as she took a ginger cookie from the silver tray. She had come for a short visit to sympathise with her family on her nephews' disappearance.

"Hope is for the hopeless. The bird might have been shot and eaten by hunters on his way to Viz. Who in his senses relies on birds nowadays? Please, Aunt Malgory, don't tell me you believe in such shit," Princess Experalda responded sarcastically.

"I don't know why, but I feel within me that they're out there somewhere," King Bruno said as he gazed out of the window, his thoughts fading into the disappearing landscape.

Nathanael knelt before Eyon, holding him tightly as tears dropped from his eyes.

"I don't want to go, Papa. I don't want to leave you and Mama by yourselves," Nathanael cried.

"My beloved son, opportunity knocks at the door when the student is ready. You've long awaited this moment, and you're ready now. It's the right time for you to leave," Eyon replied.

"No, I'm not ready. I still have much to learn from you," Nathanael insisted.

"You've learned everything you needed to know," Eyon reassured him. "It's time to put that into practise. You'll grow in strength and knowledge as you go about your duty. You don't need me anymore.

Don't be afraid to fail, because they're part of your learning. In everything, seek to become better than before.

"You shouldn't worry about us," he continued. "Mama and I shall be fine with Mikael here with us. And if one day you ever need us, just let us know and we'll be there for you," Eyon said.

"No, Papa, no. I'm afraid of the unknown. I don't know how to deal with it!" Nathanael sobbed his face soaked with tears.

"Fear is spice for challenging the unknown. Believe in yourself, my son, and just follow your instinct. You've been trained and have nurtured your power for twelve years. You'll make it. Everything is made possible as you believe, and never ignore that soft inner voice within you. It will guide you.You took care of animals in the barn, and this experience is sufficient. Simply translate what you've learned from this to whatever experience you'll face. Never look behind. Go forward, you have all our blessings," Eyon responded as tears fell from his eyes.

Nathanael kissed him several times on his forehead, hugged his grandmother, and kissed her on the forehead too. She held him tightly, murmured a few words in his ears, and kissed him again. He hugged Mikael and instructed him to take good care of their grandparents. It was an emotional moment.

As they walked out of the house towards Eyon's carriage, Nathanael turned and looked at his family one more time. He did not know if he would see them again as he bid them farewell, and they too waved back at him in front of their doorstep.

I've waited for this moment all my life and never thought leaving home would hurt so much. No turning back, no looking behind. At least I go with Wodwuck, Nathanael reflected.

Wodwuck has been his long-time eagle friend that he had nursed when he was still an eaglet and Nathanael was four. Happy that his companion had embarked with him on this journey, Nathanael projected himself into the future.

Chapter 11

Gwendoline and Her Friends

P rincess Gwendoline received her score for the regional school contest that had been organized a few weeks after midsummer. It was a yearly competition during which merit was given by awarding scholarships to deserving pupils from several kingdoms.

Among the 480 pupils from the surrounding kingdoms, Princess Gwendoline ranked second, scoring 97 per cent. Shawn, her friend from the same school, scored 100 per cent and was first in the region. Their teacher, Ms Melliby Gloria, informed them that their prizes would be handed over in two weeks.

Princess Gwendoline was not happy with her result, because her mum would bark about it. Last year she had performed better and was first; this year, she was not, and she knew her mother would blame this on her attendance at Uncle Benjamin's Friday parties, as well as her reluctance to do homework during the Royal Midsummer Festival. Though, the real reason was because the mathematics quiz was trickier this year.

After the school bell rang, she met Shawn on her way out of the classroom and congratulated him on his performance. She also invited him for a play party in the castle and asked her friend Leslie, who scored 58 per cent and ranged somewhere below in the regional list, to join them.

Princess Experalda paced across their living room on the tenth floor.

"Darling why are you restless? Is something wrong?" Robert Vincent asked.

"No, everything is fine," she replied.

"Of course nothing is fine. I know you too well," Robert said.

"Okay. There is a rumour going on that I am responsible for the disappearance of Benjamin and Bernard in order to inherit their thrones. Though I don't care what others say about me, what annoys me is the fact that it seems Mum and Bruno are suspicious of me and I don't know what future action against me they might take. Xexez, the laundry master, overheard them commenting on this," Princess Experalda said.

"But darling, why do you mind? Haven't you secretly desired that they fail? You voiced your ambition for revenge when you last conversed with your mum in her apartments. As you said, it seems as though they suspect you. This is not actually an accusation but a suspicion. They didn't come to you for that nor did they accuse you of anything – and besides, your mum and Bruno are very straightforward people who say what they think. I suppose Xexez overheard your mum mentioning to Bruno your visit to her apartment, and he simply mixed it up with the rumour going on," Robert said.

"Certainly, I had all the reason to be mad at Mum for not convening me to their last meeting, and I was equally angry at them for blindly believing this Dumbbell fool. They act so illogically and are quick to trust others, while none of them trusts me. I don't deny the fact that I expected my brothers to fail as usual in their quest for the Bearer, but I didn't wish that they get hurt or lost," she replied.

"Calm down, rumour blows away like the wind. I'm always on your side no matter what," Robert said.

While they spoke, Princess Gwendoline came in, greeted her parents, and hurried straight to her bedroom.

Some minutes later, "Gwendy, you may now come down, your lunch is served. Hurry up, it will get cold," Princess Experalda said.

"Yes, Mummy, in a minute," Princess Gwendoline replied as she came out of her bedroom, quickly placed her test results on the table where her parents sat, and then headed straight to the table without looking at them.

"Oh no, not today! Gwendy, what's this?" Princess Experalda exclaimed. "I knew something was wrong from the way you walked into this house – 97 per cent in the regional contest, and you rank second? I don't like what I see. You would've performed better if only you had concentrated on your weekend homework rather than those Friday parties and if you'd studied seriously during the midsummer festivities. Finish your meal and tell me more about this."

"Yes, Mummy," Princess Gwendoline replied, not knowing what awaited her.

"Come on, Experalda, she was second. Is that not enough? Stop stressing this child," Robert said.

"What? This is a drastic drop. For heaven's sake, she was first last year."

"Coolio, coolio, everything is all right. Be happy for her," Robert replied.

After taking as long as possible over her meal, Princess Gwendoline presented herself before her parents as requested. Her dad congratulated her, which made her smile, but her face dampened when it met her mum's stern look, which made her feel guilty.

"Sorry, Mum. I know I should have done better, and I promise that I'll be first next year. I accept any punishment you have for me," Princess Gwendoline hastily said before her mum could speak.

"It's all right, my little angel," Princess Experalda replied, softened by her daughter's words. "But I'll see to it that next year, this doesn't repeat itself."

"May I play in the garden this afternoon? My friends Shawn and Leslie will be here at four o'clock."

"Oh, sure you may," Princess Experalda replied. "Ask Margarette to prepare some tea, cake, and biscuits for your friends," she concluded.

Shawn arrived with four pink roses for Princess Gwendoline, and Leslie had apricot sweets made by her mum. Princess Gwendoline was very pleased by these presents. She introduced her friends to her parents before going off to play.

Later, in the garden, Margarette served them banana sponge cake, ginger cookies, and orange juice. By four thirty, they had finished up and were playing hide and seek in the garden. At five thirty, they searched for butterflies.

As they walked past one of the gardens, Leslie shouted, "Look, look at what I've found! Look at this beautiful bird perching on the birch tree!"

Immediately, Princess Gwendoline and Shawn turned in the direction she indicated.

"Oh, that's SpyBrow, Uncle Bernard's bird!" Princess Gwendoline exclaimed.

"Your uncle has a bird?" Shawn asked keenly.

"Yes he does. He says he's his friend, and he talks to him every day in the garden," Princess Gwendoline said.

"Then let's talk to him too!" Shawn exclaimed in excitement.

"Hope he doesn't fly away as we come closer," Leslie said.

The children drew closer to SpyBrow. He did not fly off but simply stared at them.

"Hello! Hello, SpyBrow!" Princess Gwendoline said.

"He doesn't talk back. Are you certain he can talk?" Shawn asked Gwendoline.

"Of course he does. If Uncle Bernard says so, then it's true," Princess Gwendoline replied.

"It isn't true," Leslie said.

"It is," Princess Gwendoline replied.

"It isn't. This bird doesn't talk. He just stares at us weirdly," Leslie said.

"If you go on like this, I shall not invite you next time to play," Princess Gwendoline said.

"Okay, I believe you, the bird can talk," Leslie shouted.

"Hahaha! Girls," Shawn said.

"Shuuuut up!" both girls shouted.

"Why do you shout?" SpyBrow tweeted.

The kids turned towards the bird and looked amazed. " He really talks!" they exclaimed.

"SpyBrow, I thought you were on the journey with Uncle Bernard. Why are you here?" Princess Gwendoline asked.

SpyBrow just stared at her without answering.

"Let's leave this place. This bird has irritating manners," Princess Gwendoline said.

As they turned their backs to go, Spy tweeted loudly, "King Bernard is on his way to Viz. I flew from Orebra to Viz three days ago. He is coming soon. Soon he'll be here."

The kids gasped, surprised at what the bird had said. They ran back towards the birch tree and started asking lots of questions.

"This is cute. So you actually can talk. No one ever believed Uncle Bernard when he said so, but I did. I'll tell Mum that you actually talk!" said Princess Gwendoline, excited.

"Gwendy, you were right that he can talk. Ohoooo, a talking bird. I'll be here every day after school," Leslie exclaimed.

"He says your uncle is on the way. We all know that they're lost!" Shawn said.

"Shawn is right. Your uncles are lost. My mum says your wicked mum made them disappear in the deep forest," Leslie said.

"Why does your mum call mine wicked? She doesn't know her. My mum is a strong woman who stands for what she believes. She's not wicked, tell your mum that. You heard SpyBrow, my uncles are on their way to Viz, so, they haven't disappeared as your mum falsely accuses mine. Nobody should mess with my mum, because I love her. She is my mum. No one should m-e-s-s with her," Princess Gwendoline shouted at the top of her voice.

"It's okay, Gwendy, why do you scream like that?" Leslie felt bad for having called Princess Gwendoline's mother wicked. The woman had been very kind to them when they greeted her earlier that afternoon.

"Look there, a blue butterfly! Let's catch it!" Shawn said. Immediately, the girls rejoiced and ran after it.

That evening, Princess Gwendoline recounted the afternoon's events to her mother, who found it unbelievable that SpyBrow could talk (if at all he existed). That night, as she watched her daughter sleep, she thought to herself, *This child's imagination runs wild. She has been listening too much to Bernard and misses her uncles.*

One afternoon, the two royal husbands played chess, Robert said, "I'm worried about Experalda. She is not herself these days."

"Why?" King Rowel asked.

"She thinks that Ursula and Bruno blame her for Benjamin and Bernard's disappearance. This affects her mood, and she's thinking about relocating to another kingdom where she would be more appreciated and useful," Robert replied.

"Yes, I understand. It's unfair to suspect someone without proof, but it's not in Ursula's or Bruno's nature to do so. I think she is projecting all these rumours from outside onto her mum and brother because she's frustrated by the situation she finds herself in. But you know, her intentions towards her brothers hasn't always been good, and as a proverb states, 'There is no fire without smoke.' She also has herself to blame for this," King Rowel said.

"Yes, but there is an English proverb which says that an idle brain is the devil's workshop. I think she should be given a chance in participating in royal matters of Viz. She is intelligent. Viz also needs such a monarch. This thing with her brothers is simply her response to rejection. No one acknowledges her potential," Robert said.

"Yes, perhaps you're right. I just say what I see, but I agree with you that she's bright and deserves some role in running Viz. Tell Bruno – he is the commander in chief here. The other two will easily be persuaded if he agrees to give her a chance," King Rowel said.

"Never mind. Let's continue to observe in silence as we've always done," Robert said.

"Yes, let's just observe. Nothing is better than a peaceful living. I don't want to make things hard for myself by meddling in the affairs of Viz," King Rowel concluded.

A week after this conversation, the ten top students were present with their families and friends at the award ceremony of the regional school contest, held in Viz. Thrilled at the idea of receiving gifts, maths geniuses would be granted a lifetime scholarship at the prestigious Mathematics Academy where they would later graduate as astronauts, scientists and professors.

Created many years back by Queen Ursula in collaboration with kings from the surrounding kingdoms, the event attracted crowds who acclaimed the nobles as they arrived: the hard-to-please King Mathew of Vasso; the shrewd King Keneth of Riz; the demanding Queen Nola of Basheba; the lukewarm King Lordworm of Loungland; the ambitious Queen Rita of Massive; the calm Princess Anna of Noland (representing her parents who were on a mission), the arrogant Prince Bell of Mellington, the bold King Winberg of Gothen, the notorious King Marismo of Riazon, the possessive Queen Bella of Nuthurton, the wicked King Orio of Wiz, and of course, the overbearing King Bruno of Viz, who was the host.

King Bruno sat next to King Mathew, who ignored him due to their latest clash at the birthday party and as a result of several years of unresolved feud. As the protocol ushered King Bruno to the podium to introduce the ceremony as the host, King Mathew teased him: "Don't forget to pay homage to your lost siblings, especially that confused Benjamin."

"I pity your apathy," King Bruno replied as he glanced at the man sternly.

The ceremony reached its climax with everyone forgetting whatever was displeasing to him or her – the royal feuds, the accusing rumours, the disappearance gossips, the noisy crowd, the buzzing flies, the disappointment of not being among the rewarded contestants, the dirty body smells, and any other thing which annoys people when they are gathered together.

After Shawn received his award, it was Princess Gwendoline's turn to be called onstage. As she received hers, she waved at her family who stood proudly cheering her – Princess Experalda, Prince Robert Vincent, Queen Ursula, King Rowel, and King Bruno. She beamed as she carried along her prizes, which included a certificate of recognition, a scholarship for Class 4, books, toys, colourful candies, and the prestigious certificate granting her entrance into the Mathematics Academy (once awarded, grantees could skip primary school and go straight ahead to the Academy). For the second year in a row, she received this certificate, but her mum did not want her into the Academy.

The whole of Viz was proud of both Princess Gwendoline and Shawn because they had made it to the top three. It was an affair of kingdom pride.

A vast banquet in the manner of Viz followed afterwards for the awardees and their families as well as the royal guests. The crowd loved this regional contest, particularly when Viz organised it, because it was always so grandiose, and food always overflowed.

Chapter 12

The Long-Awaited Moment

The discussions of the attendants at the award ceremony were centred around the lost brothers. It had now been nine weeks since they had left for their voyage, and were yet to return. The guests at the banquet asked the same questions to King Bruno: Did he have any news about his brothers? Some pretended as though they sympathised with him, but internally rejoiced.

At one point, exasperated by all these questions, King Bruno left for some moments of quiet. As he reflected by his most preferred window, all of a sudden, a cloud of dust approached from afar, and he exclaimed, "Here they come! Here they come! Come and see for yourselves, here they come!"

At this, the invitees rushed to the window by which he stood. Filled with enthusiasm, he ran downstairs, and they followed him behind. The sun was settling by now.

An old-looking carriage entered the castle from the backyard, where a crowd of onlookers had already gathered. It was followed by the white-armoured horse rider. As its occupants descended - Dorland, Springbell, Dumbbell, Earl, kings Benjamin and Bernard - King Bruno exclaimed joyfully, "Welcome my beloved ones, welcome back to Viz! We missed you so much and thought you were lost."

"Certainly it's nice to have you home, my dear sons and travelling companions. We thought we'd never see you again!" Queen Ursula panted as she spoke; she had run too quickly for her age. She embraced them all as she spoke.

"Good heavens!" Queen Malgory said suddenly. "You all look pale and withered. What happened?"

"Hello boys!" Princess Experalda said as she stared defiantly at her mother and King Bruno. "Happy to know that you're alive and not lost. Someone is free from unfounded suspicion."

Some guests attending the banquet who earlier had showed false sympathy excused themselves and left in a haste, including King Mathew, who could hardly look King Bruno in the eye out of shame for his previous mockery during the award ceremony.

"Did you find the Bearer?" Queen Ursula inquired eagerly.

"Oh yes, Mum," King Benjamin answered enthusiastically.

"Then where is he?" Princess Experalda demanded.

"Right *here*-," King Benjamin gestured proudly.

As King Benjamin spoke, a small boy descended from the carriage. He had with him an eagle that was gripped on his left arm. As his feet touched the ground, he raised his hands in the air, muttered some words in a strange language, and immediately, the eagle flew high into the sky and then disappeared as it screeched loud.

By this time, King Rowel and all the castle was out. Everyone marvelled at this young lad, whose presence was magnetizing. His eyes glowed like burning embers. By all evidence, he was the Bearer, though words could not explain this.

"Are you the Bearer?" King Rowel asked. "And where did that eagle fly to?"

"Yes, I am. I sent Wodwuck to inform my family of my safe arrival. It'll be back tomorrow," Nathanael said.

"Young man, what is your name?" Queen Ursula inquired.

"Nathanael Nordmark," he replied.

"Where are you from?", Princess Experalda asked just for curiosity. "I was told the Bearer is a tough warrior. You look too small for that. Are you truly the Bearer, and if yes, why have you been hiding?"

"I come from Orebra, land of the strong and wise. I wasn't hiding, I had been preparing for this day. Strength is not size but substance," he answered with authority.

"How old are you?" Princess Gwendoline asked.

"Twelve?"

"Well done, Dumbbell. We're proud of you. You've been right from the onset," Queen Ursula said.

"Till now, nothing proves that this boy is indeed the Bearer," Princess Experalda noted, displeased at the thought that she could have been wrong from the onset of this. "He should wear that Multicoloured Coat."

"You should be hungry. Let's go in," Queen Ursula said and ushered them inside.

As they chatted in the main living room, questions flew from every corner. Everyone was eager to know every detail of their journey.

"We expected you to be back in six weeks. You took eight – what went wrong? We sent help as soon as we heard from the black knight of your incident in the woods, and a search was conducted to no avail. What happened?" King Bruno asked.

At this, King Bernard related their whole venture and then concluded, "As we approached Viz, we sent Spy ahead of us as a sign that we had succeeded in finding the Bearer, as I'd promised," King Bernard said.

"Ha! We never saw any bird of that kind," exclaimed Princess Experalda. "You still believe in bird fairy tales?"

"Oh yes, we did see him, Uncle Bernard!" Princess Gwendoline interjected. "He spoke to me when I was in the garden with Shawn and Leslie."

"Never mind, birds or not, the essential thing is that we're happy you're back safe and sound," Queen Ursula said.

Some moments later, they all dined at the large table, and King Benjamin became extremely merry. "Hummm, the good life, how I missed it. I've never tasted such good wine in my entire life. Never will I ever venture into the woods again. It's too dangerous," he said as he drank more wine from his golden cup.

Everyone laughed at his words as they sat around the dining table. That evening, there was happiness in the castle of Viz as the venturers recounted their intriguing adventures.

After dinner and before retreating to bed, they all resettled in the living room. King Bruno instructed one of his staff who had acted as counsellor in the absence of Earl. "Prepare a message that would convene the citizens of Viz to the palace. Inform them that the Bearer has been found and he will be officially presented as well as wear the Multicoloured Coat. Do this tomorrow at the earliest."

"Your order is a command, my Lord," the servant responded.

The next morning, yellow-dressed messengers paraded through the city, blowing trumpets and reading King Bruno's message. That morning, King Bernard was curious about what might have happened to SpyBrow, and he went to meet the bird in his favourite garden spot.

"Hello, Bernard!" SpyBrow said.

"Hello, Spy! What have you been up to? We've scores to settle, for I'm displeased with you. You did not do as you'd been told," King Bernard said.

"I didn't do as told? Explain yourself. You look ridiculous with that wrinkled brow. Anger doesn't suit you the way it does Bruno or Experalda," SpyBrow whistled.

"Why didn't you inform my family that we'd found the Bearer and were safe and sound as we'd agreed you would do?" King Bernard asked.

"Well, let's just say I was curious to observe more of what was happening in Viz when I arrived. There were lots of rumours about your disappearance, and Princess Experalda became so disturbed by rumors blaming her for your disappearance. She thought your mum and King Bruno suspected her for that. There was so much interesting gossip in town about this subject that I decided to become invisible and follow everything through without intervening to see how things would turn out," SpyBrow said.

"That was not kind of you. Didn't you pity my old mum who had been worried for so long? Did you reflect on the consequences of your action?" King Bernard asked.

"Yes, I did. Well, let's say my action was just very few days away from your arrival, and it wouldn't have changed an ounce of your mum's worry. Besides, I knew that the more people gossiped, the more your coming would be glorious, and so I chose to let things be," SpyBrow tweeted happily.

"Bad bird, you're full of mischief," King Bernard said.

"Forgive me, Lord Bernard, for being a bad bird. Next time, I will be a good one," SpyBrow said. "Twee twee twee twee twee twee twee! Friends now, okay, lovely King Bernard?" he whistled teasingly.

The following day, by eleven o'clock as had been announced, an excited crowd stood before the kings, queens, and castle staff. King Bruno made a speech and praised the courageous travellers as he recounted their acts of bravery. He quickly concluded, "The long-awaited moment has now arrived for us to know if Nathanael is indeed the Bearer. Bring the Multicoloured Coat!" he gestured ceremoniously.

Nathanael, who had been stroking Wodwuck's feathers, approached. As he held the coat in his hand, the eagle flew to a close balcony decorated with colorful flags. Everywhere was still. The air was calm and no insect dared to sing.

At first view, the coat looked very big for Nathanael, and it was obvious that it wouldn't fit. As he put it on enthusiastically, however, to everyone's surprise, it fitted perfectly. Speechless, everyone gazed with mouths open.

Just like in my visions, Nathanael thought.

How could such a big coat suddenly become small? Princess Experalda thought. She could not comprehend it with her logical mind. *Indeed, he is the Bearer,* she admitted to herself.

"Dear people of Viz," said King Bruno, "count yourselves blessed among the living. You've witnessed with your very own eyes this day the long-awaited Bearer. Myths have been told about him for ages, and today we all have the privilege of seeing this myth come true. Go home and rest assured that life will be better for us all from now henceforth. Good is coming to Viz," King Bruno said in conclusion.

News ran across kingdoms that the Bearer had been found.

Before going to bed, Queen Ursula called for a secret meeting in the Russian Roulette room with kings Bruno, Benjamin, Bernard, and Rowel, plus Queen Malgory, Earl, Ingrid, and Dumbbell. She had called for this short meeting because she was so eager to learn what the Book of Prophecies had in store for Viz.

Before the meeting commenced, Princess Experalda walked into the room. "You didn't think you'd hold such an important meeting without me. Not this time around. I heard news of your plans."

"Experalda, please, may I ask you to leave, for this concerns kingdom matters which are of no interest to you," Queen Ursula said.

"Oh yes they are. Any kingdom matter concerns any citizen of Viz, and I am one. Moreover, I belong to the noble bloodline, which makes me all the more welcome to this secret meeting, whether it pleases you or not. Sorry, I'm so comfortably seated, and it will be difficult for me to leave," Princess Experalda said, settling into a chair.

Queen Ursula stared at her for a while and then continued: "I convened this meeting because I want Ingrid to hand over the Book of Prophecies to Nathanael. We'd been told that he alone could read it and interpret its strange sounds."

As Ingrid handed the book over, she said, "My dad, Ingerman Vong Wickstrom, advised me for Viz's sake to safely secure the Book of Prophecies until the Bearer was found, or until I found someone reliable to pass it on to, if I hadn't witnessed the Bearer's discovery. My joy cannot be explained as I hand it over to you, Nathanael. At this moment, I bestow on you the responsibility of keeper of the Book of Prophecies and the guardian to the Ancestral Treasure Room," she said, her voice trembling with mixed feelings.

Nathanael took the book and quickly swept across its pages front to back.

"Tell us, Nathanael, what're these strange sounds? Are you able to read anything from the blank pages? We're so anxious," Queen Ursula said.

"These sounds are the words written in the Book of Prophecies. The pages aren't blank but rather full of writings. On page 439 I read, 'The Canopy is a door to the Door. It brings into existence the unseen and provides you with a share of your belief,'" Nathanael said.

"Show me, where is that written," King Bernard asked, amazed beyond words, for though he was close to Nathanael, he could not see a thing but only a bare page.

"It's from this page, 439, do you see?" Nathanael pointed towards the page, not having grasped the fact that he alone could see its writings.

"Nathanael, no one else sees the writings but you. These pages are blank," Princess Experalda emphasized.

"Read page 500," King Bruno said.

"'Beneath the sun sits three diamond stones. Forgone are the days of the moon's bright and its glory should be restored. The one with unshaved hair is the key,'" Nathanael continued.

"What about page 1?" King Benjamin inquired.

"'Dreams were realities and mankind pains were eased,'" Nathanael read.

"What about page 2?" Princess Experalda inquired.

"'He stands on the shoulders of giants and through him, they will see.'"

"Do you know the significance of these parables?" Queen Ursula asked.

"Yes, I do. The pages I just read signify this: a long time ago, there existed a perfect world wherein people had no burdens. Their dreams became reality through the Dream Sofa. This Dream Sofa was found in Viz and served as a cradle for life for many. It also kept order not only in this kingdom but in several. Through an ill fate, three kings entitled to its protection were defiled. The three diamond stones refer to kings Bruno, Benjamin, and Bernard, whose greatness has been darkened by an evil enchantment that can only be broken when the Dream Sofa returns to Viz. The empowered Bearer is to help them restore their lost glory, and all three kings are predestined for a long journey in quest of that Dream Sofa, which when brought back to Viz, will enable them enjoy their reign as it is meant to be. I am the unshaved hair who is to help them in this quest," Nathanael said.

"Holy Saint. Nooooo, not another journey," King Benjamin exclaimed in horror at the thought of travelling again.

"Enchanted, we? How come and for what reason? Mum, did you know about this?" King Bernard asked as the three brothers turned towards her for an answer.

"I heard something of that sort but didn't believe it till now that the prophecy ascertains it. Rumour has it that this spell is responsible for your weird behaviour as kings. That said, I think you should all focus on your next assignment, my dear boys. Any additional questions regarding the enchantment should be addressed to the Bearer. Good night," Queen Ursula concluded.

During the months that followed, the triplet kings and Nathanael prepared for their long journey in quest of the Dream Sofa, which was hidden in an unknown land. Nathanael read and meditated through every passage of the Book of Prophecies and went about the discovery of secrets found in the Ancestral Treasure Room. He searched for every bit of information that would equip him for their challenge.

King Bernard prepared too by rereading every book in the library and questioning Nathanael daily on any new revelation he had from the Book of Prophecies. This book could foretell, when it wanted to, anything about anyone.

King Bruno arranged for the travel logistics, while King Benjamin, seemingly unworried, chatted a lot with Dumbbell, whose knowledge on riddles led to his engagement as the librarian of the castle's library. Dumbbell had discovered, with the help of King Bernard, that Ingrid was his sister; Bernard had attentively listened to his childhood story and smartly made the link with Ingrid. Dumbbell told everyone that his real name was Orion Vong Wickstrom and that part of the reason he travelled extensively was in search of his half-siblings. He and Ingrid had so many years to catch up on, though this would not occur since she passed away some months after. He learned that Winter had been expelled from Viz for treason.

Nathanael grew in wisdom as he read from cover to cover of the Book of Prophecies. He knew what awaited them in this perilous journey across an unknown land.

Once again, Viz was to experience the reign of a woman: that of Princess Experalda, who would serve as acting Queen of Viz in the absence of her brothers while they sought their destiny. Opportunity knocks when the student is ready.

To be continued ...

The Dream Sofa lies in Rönneshytta, Sweden, at Mama Ann-Cathrine and Papa Rikki's home.

Thank you! I hope you enjoyed this story. Watch out for part two of this series: *The Bearer, the Dream Sofa, and The Journey.*

CPSIA information can be obtained
at www.ICGtesting.com
Printed in the USA
BVOW11*0948160317
478587BV00003B/9/P